OUTLAW JUSTICE

Keller turned away and climbed back onto his horse. His heart was hammering, and he sweated like he had just finished a fast run up a steep hill. He knew what would happen now, and that once it happened, he would undeniably be the very thing he had sworn never to be. A vigilante. An Old Boy. He couldn't back out now. So be it.

Doyle Boston threw his rope over the limb and tied a noose. A couple of others in the group joined him with ropes of their own. The three horse thieves watched the process wordlessly; the first had gotten control of himself and now only whimpered a little. Keller was glad the man had stopped his crying.

Keller didn't want to watch the actual hanging, but he made himself do it. Having come this far, he wouldn't falter.

BRAZOS

Cameron Judd

BANTAM BOOKS

NEW YORK • TORONTO • LONDON • SYDNEY • AUCKLAND

BRAZOS

A Bantam Domain Book / March 1994

ISBN 0-553-56550-8

Published simultaneously in the United States and Canada

Bantam Books are published by Bantam Books, a division of
Bantam Doubleday Dell Publishing Group, Inc. Its trademark,
consisting of the words "Bantam Books" and the portrayal of a
rooster, is Registered in U.S. Patent and Trademark Office and
in other countries. Marca Registrada. Bantam Books, 1540
Broadway, New York, New York 10036.

PRINTED IN THE UNITED STATES OF AMERICA

RAD   0 9 8 7 6 5 4 3 2

"Lightnin' Les," this one's for you.

Aspects of this story were initially suggested by certain historical events that took place in and around Fort Griffin, Texas, in the 1870s. But initial suggestion is as far as it went. This story is not a disguised depiction of any events or characters out of Texas history, but is entirely a work of fiction.

BRAZOS

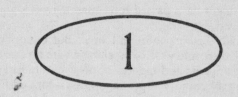

1

The first man stood alone in the late winter dusk. Before him were two graves that still bore the indentations of the shovels that had dug and filled them many days before.

The graves were marked with wood crosses and lay near the place the house had stood. The house itself was now nothing but a pile of thoroughly burned, stinking timber. The fire must have raged every bit as hot as the folks in nearby Cade had declared, for the ground for several yards all around was blackened even yet, the chimney had crumbled to a rubble heap from the heat, and two nearby outbuildings had also burned to the ground. The little cookhouse and adjacent bunkhouse stood on the other side of a narrow grove of trees, out of sight and far enough away that they had been spared destruction.

Hat in hand, the mackinawed man stood by Magart Broadmore's final resting place and wondered morbidly how anyone had managed to find any human remains worthy of burial after such a conflagration.

He was a tall man in his forties, broad-shouldered and long-legged. Unlike his smooth-pated father, who had balded in his twenties, he had managed so far to keep every bit of the thick shock of hair that curled behind his ears, despite all his efforts to comb it straight. It was gray at the temples, but the rest remained black as nightshade. If not for his thoroughly weather-creased face, he might have passed for a man ten years younger than he was.

Usually he was calm and stoic. But today he was deeply shaken, and glad to be alone where no one could see the dampness and redness of his eyes. He had come to the Brazos country expecting to find a long-estranged sister. He had not come expecting to find her and her husband dead, and their ranch abandoned.

His moistened eyes shifted to the other grave, the one closest to the ruins of the house, the one marked F. R. BROADMORE—b. 1842, d. 1875. His lip curled in distaste that approached hatred. He harbored no grief for this grave's occupant. Folly Broadmore had been a sorry soul in life, and death did nothing to make the thought of him any more tolerable. The man was born no good and had lived up to his heritage. Gambler, cheat, sometime swindler, full-time loser. That was Folly Broadmore.

Too bad they were already buried when I got here, the man thought. *I never would have let them bury Magart beside him. It ain't right that she has to lie beside a man like him, even if he was her husband.*

He turned away, eyes sweeping the rolling Brazos country. He dug a hand under his coat and into his pocket to fetch out his tobacco and papers. Within a few seconds he had rolled a perfect cigarette, or quirly, as he would have called it. Snapping a phosphorus-and-sulfur match off the match block in his pocket, he struck flame on his boot heel and lit the tobacco. The smoke of it was raw against his throat, but it soothed him.

The sun, swollen and orange, was nestling its lower edge against the western horizon. The wind rose higher, carrying the scent of river and town through the chill-sharpened air. The man sniffed. Funny thing, he mused, how that lousy town seemed to have its own distinct scent, like a living thing. He could pick it out from here, a full two miles away. It was a conglomerate smell of humans, horses, dogs, pigs, cattle, timber, chimney smoke, tobacco, whiskey, and all the thousand other things that went into the mix of the ugly little farrago that had grown up in the shadow of equally ugly Fort Cade.

The man tossed down the quirly and crushed it under his heel. Putting foot to stirrup, he swung into his gelding's saddle and rode slowly by the light of the sunset back toward Cade. There was only one thing to do at a time like this: Get as drunk as possible, and stay that way as long as he could.

The second man wasn't as tall as the first, but every bit as lean, perhaps leaner. His hair was wispy, thinning on the crown of his head, and its color was that of wet sand. His skin was fair, more freckled and windburnt than tan.

He was crouched in the brush beside a curving stream that snaked between two low hills wooded with oak. Above him hung an orange and violet sunset. He held a battered carbine, already levered and cocked, and his heart thumped like a hammer. A little rivulet of blood stained his calf, coming from a superficial bullet wound suffered while he rode full tilt away from the three horsemen who had pursued him.

He hadn't recognized any of the three and hoped they hadn't recognized him. Who were they? Ranchers, cowboys . . . or range detectives? He hoped not the latter, though the possibility was there. Local ranchers were getting weary of losing stock, and drastic measures, such as hired range guards, could not be too long in coming.

He shifted his posture and winced at the pain of his wound. Glancing at it, he wondered how deep it was. The pain of it was certainly noticeable, though there was not the dull throb of a deep puncture. It had been a grazing shot, nothing more. But he would have to get rid of these bloodied trousers, for a bloodstained and bullet-torn fabric would generate some uncomfortable questions back in Cade.

He crouched where he was for the next half hour. Finally, when it was almost fully dark, he stood, grinning broadly. No pursuers had appeared; they must have gone past on the far side of the rise. He spoke to the black horse that searched for early forage behind him, down by the water and out of sight of any potential watchers from the rolling countryside beyond the oak stand. "Horse, I think we shook 'em."

He examined his wound; as he had thought, it was superficial. It had already quit bleeding on its own. The sting was gone now, leaving only a slight ache. Limping a little, he got the horse, mounted, and rode out of the thicket, heading east toward his big ranch house.

Cheerful though he was at evading capture, the experience had sobered him. He would have to be more careful in the future. He had too much going for him here in Cade to be careless. Too many plans, too many ambitions, too much to lose—and lose it all he would, if ever he was pegged as a stock thief. From here on out, he decided, he would have to leave the actual act of stock theft to his associates in crime. From now on he would play his role strictly in the background, carefully hiding the vital secret of his involvement. This would be especially important after the election was over and he was firmly ensconced in the county sheriff's office over in Cade.

On his way back to his big stone house, the man rode across the Broadmore spread. He paused there, looking toward the black rubble heap of the house. There was just enough light for him to make out the two crosses on the graves. He eyed them a moment, then rode on.

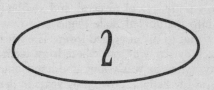

2

Two Days Later

Paco the Mex saw his beloved one drawing near. He stirred where he lay, eyes closed, and smiled. "Bellina," he whispered worshipfully. Bellina of the mysterious darkness, Bellina of eyes and hair black as midnight, Bellina of brown skin as cool to Paco's touch as the bottle of whiskey that had given her the only reality she now possessed.

"Paco . . . *hermoso, fuerte* . . ." Her voice was musical and sweet, soothing to hear, even if only in his imagination.

Only when Paco was drunk did Bellina come to him, and as far as he was concerned, that provided the best of many good reasons to get drunk as frequently as possible. When he was sober, all life had to offer was the squalor of this town: its dirt, poverty, heat, danger, and a populace that looked down on him and made him look down on himself. When he was drunk, things were better. Intoxication gave Paco the only two luxuries he had known for many years: escape from ugly reality, and Bellina, a lover made of memories and dreams.

Yet now, as Bellina reached out to caress him, her

5

touch was not a phantom's, but solid, human. A thrill shivered through Paco. She was real! She was alive! "Bellina, bella Bellina . . ." He smiled broadly, reaching out to her as he opened his eyes.

Paco's body jerked upward and suddenly he was looking into a stubbled male anglo face that was certainly not that of his imagined lover. The Mexican's lip curled back over a wide gap where front teeth had been in the days when he was young and handsome and had loved a real-life Bellina, now many years in her grave. A gargling, panicked sound bubbled up from his throat.

"Bellina, eh?" the anglo said. His eyes were red and his breath heavy with whiskey. Paco was face upward, his liquor-weakened legs, all one and a half of them, sprawled out. He had removed his whittled peg leg for comfort's sake before settling down to drink; now it lay beside him. His torso was pulled half upright as the anglo held him by the collar of his ragged coat. "I'm a long way from being any Bellina, *amigo*. You're the one they call Paco the Mex?"

"*Si, si*—I am Paco. *Misericordia, señor*, mercy . . ."

"They tell me you're a cheap thief and beggar, Paco. That right?"

"No, *señor*—*no lo quiera Dios!* I am no thief. I beg you, let me go!"

"You're a pitiful excuse even for what you are, Paco. The smell of you alone is enough to make a man sick. You think any sweet Bellina would have anything to do with a skunk like you? Do you?"

"No, *señor*. No. I am a wretch, *señor*. *Por favor*, don't hurt me!"

"Hurt you? Why would I want to hurt you? Of course, if you decide to be uncooperative . . ."

"What do you want of me, *señor*?"

"I want you to tell me what you know about the death of Magart Broadmore."

Paco suddenly recognized the man who held him.

His tongue swiped out; his eyes grew wide, making the brown-black pupils stand out against the background of the surrounding bloodshot whites. "Keller!" he said. "You are Keller!"

"That's right, Paco. I am Keller, and before she married, Magart Broadmore was named Keller too. She was my sister, Paco. I came here to find her, and what I found instead was her grave. Now I hear whispers in the saloons that you know more about how she died than what the local rag wrote."

"No! I know nothing!"

"Only a dead man knows nothing, Paco, and if you don't talk, dead you'll be. Tell me what you know about Magart Broadmore's death!"

"The fire, she died in a fire, she and her husband!"

Keller swore and shook the Mexican. "Tell me what I don't already know! Tell me the truth!"

"*Señor, por favor,* I know nothing more! I swear it before God, before the blessed Virgin! I know nothing!"

"That's not what I hear, Paco. They tell me you talk too much when you're drunk. They tell me you say it wasn't the accident it was claimed to be!"

"Please, *Señor* Keller, believe me—if I knew anything, I would tell you!"

Keller's face became hard and ugly. He was driven by liquor and fury, a state he was unaccustomed to, and therefore could hardly control. His lips tightened to a line. "You're a liar, Paco. A liar and a scoundrel. And letting you keep on breathing is a waste of good air."

Keller drew his pistol and thrust it into Paco's face. He was thumbing back the hammer when he suddenly froze, realizing the horrible thing he was about to do. *God help me, have I sunk so low as to murder a man in an alley?*

Paco wrenched free and screamed in terror as he fell back, spreading his arms behind him to catch himself. In so doing, he chanced to put his fingers around the peg leg. He grabbed it, swung it up, and clubbed

Keller soundly in the side of the head. The pistol went off in Keller's hand, splattering a harsh powder burn across the left side of Paco's face but sending the slug into the ground beside him.

The Mexican hit Keller again, knocking him aside, then leaped to his single foot. Still yelling frightfully, he began hopping away, peg leg in hand. He bounced off around the corner of the stable behind which the encounter had occurred. Keller was on his knees, grimacing and slightly dizzy from being clouted. He picked up his pistol and held it limply. "God, I almost murdered a man!" he murmured to himself. He gingerly touched his head where Paco had struck him and found blood on his fingers when he took them away.

Keller stood waveringly, pistol dangling in hand, and heard footfalls on the side of the building opposite where Paco had just run. He turned as two wide-eyed men with identical deputy badges and almost identical faces emerged to face him. One already had his pistol drawn; the other drew his as soon as he saw Keller standing there with weapon in hand.

"Drop that pistol! Drop it!" the first man ordered. Keller had seen these lawmen before and knew they were the Polk twins, Homer and Haman, look-alike brothers who helped the county sheriff ride herd on the town of Cade and its surrounding environs. Which was Homer and which was Haman, he didn't know.

Keller stooped and laid the pistol on the ground. Standing, he lifted his hands. A thin trickle of blood edged down under his collar.

"Who were you shooting at?" the lead Polk demanded, pistol still trained on Keller.

"Nobody," Keller said. His anger had drained out, replaced by shame and desperation. He wanted badly to turn and run.

"That's a lie. I heard yelling."

"That was me," Keller said, groping for an out. "I

saw a snake, yelled, and shot at it. Snakes scare me bad."

"I heard Paco the Mex's voice back here," the second Polk said. "And I don't think no snake clouted you in the skull."

"Look, men, I'm a longtime peace officer myself, and this looks to me like a situation you ought to just let drop," Keller said, flashing what he hoped was a disarming grin.

"I reckon you would think that way," the first Polk said. He squinted. "Hey, you're that Keller fellow, ain't you? Brother of poor old Magart Broadmore?"

"I am. How do you know me?"

Polk cleared his throat, looking ill at ease. "The sheriff said you were in town. I'm sorry about what happened to your sister, Mr. Keller. I feel sorry for you and all. But I can't let you go until we know what was going on back here."

Another man came around behind the Polks. "Haman, Paco the Mex just hopped all the way down the street with one side of his face burnt red, yelling he'd been shot at. He looked drunk, but he was hopping like a dang jackrabbit."

"So that *was* Paco I heard yelling back here!" Haman Polk declared. "You lied to us, Mr. Keller. Come on. Let's go see Sheriff Cooke."

"Wait a minute . . . did you say Cooke?"

"Yeah. Till Cooke. He says he knows you. Planned to look you up while you were in town. It looks like we'll be saving him the trouble. Now come on, get moving."

Keller walked all the way to the sheriff's office with Haman Polk's pistol trained on the small of his back, his hands uplifted to shoulder level, and a stunned expression on his face. Till Cooke was the law in Cade? He hadn't known that. It was the first good thing he had heard since arriving here.

Or maybe it wasn't so good. How would Till

Cooke react to learning that a man he had trained in the ways of the law had fallen to the point of beating on peg-legged Mexicans in back alleys?

This one was going to be difficult to explain, especially to a stern law-and-order man like Till Cooke.

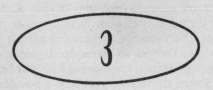

3

The Next Morning

Till Cooke had once stood five inches above six feet
tall—an imposing height that had caused many a
violence-prone drunk to choose discretion once
faced with the towering lawman. But the years had done
their work on him, arching his spine and robbing almost
three inches from his stature, while adding them, plus
many others, to his girth. Cooke's jowls had stretched
and drooped, his hair had faded to white, and his once-
erect shoulders had rounded off like weather-worn
boulders.

He took a final pull on the cigar that had rested on
his lip since breakfast. It had been lighted, allowed to go
out, and relighted all morning, until now only an inch of
it remained. Cooke flipped the butt into the belly of the
stove in the corner of the office, stretched, and ad-
dressed Haman Polk, who was seated on the corner of
the big paper-piled rolltop situated off center in the office.

"So old Jed's got himself arrested, huh?"

Haman Polk used his official voice, deeper and
cleaner-clipped than his usual slur. He and his brother

were young men, recently hired, and still stood in awe of their seasoned superior. "Yes sir, Mr. Cooke. Somebody told him that Paco the Mex has been talking about the fire that killed his sister, and Keller got drunk and decided to try to scare Paco into talking. Keller swears he didn't intend to fire a shot. Says it was an accident."

"I see. Did Paco file a complaint against Keller?"

"Oh, no. He was so scared he denied it ever happened, once we started questioning him. But he was seen hopping scared down the street with a powder burn on his face, so we know it happened. Homer tracked him down. He was hiding behind the rain barrel in the alley beside the Big Dakota."

Till Cooke said, "I'm going back to talk to Keller."

"He's sleeping."

"Then I'll wake him up." He gave a snorting chuckle. "I expected to see Jed while he was in town, but I didn't expect it would be like this."

Jed Keller was asleep on his back on the cell bunk, his hands behind his head. The cell's pillow had been ripped to pieces by a drunk who had occupied this cell the previous night, and it was now nothing but cloth and feathers all over the floor. Keller had been allowed to keep his hat, and it rested on his forehead, tipped down to shade his eyes. The only other occupant of the jail was in an adjoining cell separated from Keller's by a stone wall, and he was also asleep.

Till Cooke left the cell door open and walked over to the bunk. The cell was chilly. He crossed his arms and studied the reclining prisoner. Keller moved a little, then reached up to push back the hat enough to let him see.

"Dog if it ain't really you after all, Till," Keller mumbled sleepily. "Just like them twins said. How you doing?"

"Tolerably well, Jed," the lawman said. "Keeping myself out of hot water, which is better than I can say for you."

Keller flipped the hat off onto the floor and sat up, groaning as morning-after discomforts hit him. He yawned and stretched very slowly. "I've stepped in it this time, I admit, and I'm ashamed. I was drunk. Wouldn't have done it otherwise." He froze in mid-stretch as he got his first good look at the sheriff. "Dang, Till, you're old!"

"I am, no denying. I ain't got a day younger since I seen you last. Now, why don't you scoot over and give a tired old man a chance to rest his backside, huh?"

The bunk creaked under the added weight. Till Cooke sighed, dug a new cigar from his vest pocket and bit the end off it. For the sake of his personal budget he allowed himself only two good cigars a day. If he needed smokes beyond that, he made do with the foul-smelling "short sixes" they sold for a penny in the saloons.

After he had fired up, he reached into his pocket and handed a cigar to Keller. It was one of his good ones.

"I'm sorry about Magart," Cooke said through the rich smoke. "It's a hard thing to lose kin."

"I didn't even know she was dead until I got here," Keller said. He chuckled ironically. "Funny, in a way. You come to make peace with your sister after too many years, and find out she's dead and gone. Ain't that just the way things go!"

"Unfortunately it is." Another drag and puff. "Was it because of Magart you were pestering Paco the Mex?"

"Yeah. I heard he had been talking about a secret he knew, a secret concerning the Broadmore fire."

"Where'd you hear that?"

"A gent in a saloon. He said Paco had tried to sell him the secret in exchange for a bottle. The fellow told him no sale."

"Likely that fellow was just one of Paco's many

antagonists. He's sort of the village idiot, you know. Folks like to give him a hard time."

"So you don't think Paco really knew anything?"

"Generally speaking, Paco don't know beans from bullets. He's half crazy from drinking his life away, and makes up all kinds of stories, most as wild as weeds. Folks like to pick on him, just to make him squeal so they can have a good laugh. Life is hard for that poor old Mexican." Cooke's cigar sent him into a coughing fit. He hacked into his hand, cutting off conversation a few seconds. He cleared his throat and went on, now in a more somber tone. "Jed, I wish you hadn't have shot at Paco. It makes it look like you were sure 'nough wanting to kill him."

"It was an accident. He hit me with that wooden leg and made the pistol go off. Like I said, I wouldn't have done any of it if I hadn't been drunk."

"If you'd killed him, that would have been murder. And I would have seen you prosecuted—even if you were the best Missouri deputy I ever hired."

"I know. You'd hang your own father if he stole a horse, Till."

"Speaking of fathers, how's yours?"

"He's dead, Till."

"Mark is dead? I'm sorry to hear it. How long?"

"A month or so. It was a natural death. He was just old and wore out." Jed paused. "And he never forgave Magart for marrying Folly Broadmore. Took the anger to his grave. That's the main reason I decided to come look her up. A family ought not fight amongst itself. I wanted to patch up all the old wounds with her."

"Must have been quite a kick in the gut to get here and find out what had happened to her."

"Yeah." Keller looked sidewise at Till Cooke. Now that he was past the surprise of seeing how the years had weathered the man, he seemed more like the Till Cooke he had known when he was a neophyte deputy in Missouri, and Cooke, then his boss, was still ranked among the toughest of the frontier lawmen. "What do *you* know about that fire, Till?"

Cooke shrugged. "No more than anybody else. It started around the fireplace, as most do, and burned the house to the ground with Magart and Folly still inside. Both bodies were found. Now they're buried together in the yard. It was an accidental thing, as best anybody can tell. It's mighty sad; the Broadmore ranch was turning into a good spread."

"Was Folly good to Magart?"

"I won't lie to you, Jed. He wasn't. They say he treated her pretty rough."

Keller ground his teeth and mentally cursed Folly Broadmore's name.

"Let me give you some advice, Jed, not as sheriff to prisoner, but as one old friend to another. Go ahead and grieve for Magart, go ahead and hate Folly Broadmore for being what he was to her—but then put it aside and forget about it. You can't change a thing that's happened, and you can't let yourself get into such a state that you go around Cade pulling pistols on poor old Mexicans and such. You do any more of that, and I'll have to start interfering something fierce in your life."

"Hah! You've already interfered, it appears to me. You've got me locked up, ain't you?"

"Not anymore. You're free to go—but you heed my warning, hear? Let it go. She's dead, and nothing you can do will bring her back."

Jed Keller nodded, saying nothing.

Till Cooke stood. "How long until you're moving on, Jed?"

"I'm not," Keller replied. "Folly Broadmore had no living kin to leave that ranch to. So it appears I'm in the ranching business."

Till Cooke's brows flicked. "You—a rancher?"

"That's right," Keller replied.

"That's going to be quite a rebuilding job. You got any capital to work with?"

"I sold Pap's farm, and that property of his near Liberty. I've got more money than I've ever had, and it's already in the bank." Keller paused. "Pap had written Magart out of his will, but it was my intention to divide the inheritance with her anyway. I was too late. Too blasted late."

"I wonder if you know what you're in for, getting into the cattle business at Cade."

"It don't take any more brains than I've got to run livestock, I don't reckon."

"Things ain't been the best for ranchers here the past year or so. Or for sheriffs either . . . not that I have to worry about that part of it much longer."

"What do you mean?"

"Cade is full of every kind of scoundrel, and the whole blasted territory is crawling with stock rustlers. I've had my fill of fighting it. I've already given my notice—a few more weeks and I'm out. I'm a cattleman on the side, you know. Nothing big and no full-time hands. It's a small spread a couple of miles from Fort Cade. I'm going to devote the rest of my days to minding my own business and trying to keep the thieves out of my stock. Claire's been staying there with me, by the way."

"Claire? That skinny runt niece of yours?"

"Oh, but she's no runt now. She's pretty as a Georgia peach. She's the daughter this old widower never had a chance to have. She's really brightened up things around here for me."

"How'd she come to be with you?"

"Well, she got married right after her folks died. It was sort of like Magart's case: She didn't marry well. Her husband ran around on her and finally deserted her flat out. She divorced him. It caused quite a scandal back home. I wrote her that she was welcome to come here and rest it out, and she did. It don't appear she has any plans to leave now."

"Well, I'll be! I'd sure like to see her."

"You will—I want you out for supper tomorrow night."

"Why, thank you. I'll be there. But tell me something: Who's going to be the law about Cade, once Till Cooke throws away his badge?"

"That's up to the voters. There'll be a special election." He grinned. "Maybe you ought to run, Jed."

"No," Keller said firmly. "Not me. Let somebody else keep the peace and chase the scoundrels. I'm through with all that. I'll not see another innocent person dead by my hand." And then it struck him how ironic that statement was, given that he had come so close to killing Paco the Mex. It gave him a chill.

Till Cooke lifted his brows. "So you still won't let go of that one old tragedy, huh? Even after all these years you won't quit dwelling on it?"

Keller looked away. "It ain't that I dwell on it," he said. "It's just that it won't quit dwelling on me."

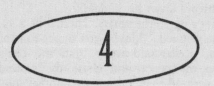

4

A nd that night it dwelled on him even more painfully
than usual. Keller sat alone in his room in the Big
Dakota Hotel, a glass and bottle of whiskey on the
table before him, and played it all through his mind for
what seemed the ten thousandth time.

It was an old memory, but no less stark for age. A
few years ago he would have tried to block it; now he let
it flow freely, knowing from experience that any other
course was futile.

He had been a fledgling Missouri deputy when it
happened. Till Cooke, then in his strapping prime, had
hired him only a month before, and Jed Keller was still
operating under a full head of pride-generated steam.
He felt he cut quite the dashing figure when he strode
the streets in his brand-new gun belt and badge. The
badge had been well-worn from use by half a dozen
previous deputies, but Keller had shined it up nicely and
enjoyed catching the flash of it in the bottom of his eye
when it glinted in the sunlight.

The first days on the job had been easy. Then came
the first major challenge for the young peace officer:
nothing less than an armed robbery of a bank. It had
occurred on an autumn afternoon so quiet that at the

beginning the entire thing seemed surreal. Keller remembered running with Till Cooke from the marshal's office toward the bank, holding a rifle snatched from the rack and feeling that surely this was all a jest or misunderstanding.

As Keller and Cooke came into sight of the bank, the sound of a gunshot and the appalling sight of a man's body flopping limply out a side window brought home the reality and horror of what was happening. Later inquiry would reveal that the dead man was a teller who had bolted toward the open window and took a bullet for his efforts. He had expired even as he lunged out the window onto the street.

That killing was the start of a long standoff with the robbers, who remained inside the bank, holding hostages. Cooke deputized townsmen on the spot and sent them scurrying to fetch rifles, and at length a charge against the bank was made. In the course of the foray many shots were fired on all sides, and when it was done, the three robbers were in custody, and Jed Keller stood looking down on the body of the first man he had ever killed.

He was little more than a boy. A simple fellow in his early twenties, who kept the bank swept for a few pennies a week. In the confusion Keller had mistaken him for one of the robbers and gunned him down. The moment when he realized his terrible error, an unforgettable feeling churned through him. For a long time thereafter Keller would awaken at night, reliving that same sickening burst of horror, feeling it chew through his insides like some parasitic worm.

That had been so many years ago, and still that feeling would come from time to time, making him waken covered with chilly sweat.

Only the gentle counsel of Till Cooke had stopped Jed Keller from ending his career in law enforcement right after the shooting. Things like that happen to the best of us, Cooke had told him. Someday it might happen to me, or maybe again to you. You can't let it stop your work. Where there's law to be upheld, there's always the risk of mistakes. But for every mistake you make, no matter how big it is, you'll do a score of things right. For every life wrongfully taken in the name of law, there are a score rightfully saved.

Keller had listened, and in the end decided not to resign. He had stayed on with Cooke, building his skills and rebuilding his confidence, eventually going elsewhere, to other Missouri towns and jobs, but always as a peace officer of one kind or another. He had never known anything else, except for some meager farming and cattle work on the side.

Though Till Cooke's counsel had been enough to keep him a lawman, it hadn't erased the haunting memory of the wrongful shooting at the bank. Even now, Jed Keller remembered the way that poor fellow had looked, dead and bloodied on the floor. And for the past two years, for some reason, the memory had grown even more clear and came more frequently. At the same time, Keller had found it increasingly difficult to do his job well, for every time he had to draw his pistol to quiet some rowdy cowboy or threatening drunk, he would for a second see in their features the face of that dead boy in the bank.

Keller poured another glass of whiskey and lifted it toward his lips, then in a burst of self-disgust threw it against the wall. Whiskey splattered in an amber explosion and dripped down the wallboards. *What am I trying to do,* he thought, *turn myself into a drunk? What good would that do?*

Keller decided he needed a walk and what fresh air the smelly environs of Cade had to offer. He stood, swiftly donned hat and mackinaw, and stalked out of his room, taking care to lock the door. Stowed in the wardrobe were the few personal possessions he had brought with him to Cade. Most of what he owned had been sold along with his father's holdings, for he had wanted to make a thoroughly fresh start.

Keller strode through the streets and examined the town. Since coming here he had been too distracted by his sister's death to take a close look at Cade. Now that he did, he was impressed, and not positively.

The town was ugly and haphazard, splattered across the flat below the hill on which Fort Cade stood. About every other building was a saloon, dance hall, gambling house, or liquor store. On the sagging balconies of several buildings women in bright, tight-fighting dresses postured provocatively and blew inviting kisses at the men on the street below. Keller, as a good-looking newcomer, got plenty of such attention. He ignored it. He liked women as well as any man, but not this kind of woman. He had been married once before, to a fine and beautiful young lady. Like a fool, he had let her slip away. But her memory had spoiled him. He had no use for cheap women who were bought for a night and cast aside.

He smiled ironically as he walked, thinking how odd an expectation of Cade he had held before actually seeing the town. As he had nursed his ailing father through the last months of his life, vainly urging him to put aside his animosity toward his estranged daughter, Keller had begun to think of coming to Cade to find Magart and set things right again. He had pictured Cade as a place of refuge, a quiet town that would likely be filled with flowers and beauty and peace. It was a strange and baseless way to think, but still the notion had lingered and grown into a firm and detailed illusion.

Now that he was here, the illusion was crumbling like dried mud. If Cade was a refuge at all, it was a refuge for lost souls.

True, there were a handful of tame and common institutions—a post office, jail, large general store, bakery, laundry, dress shop, feed store, and even a church house shared by the Catholics and the Presbyterians—but these were so overshadowed by the various houses of vice that they blended almost invisibly into the dingy background. This was a mud-colored town on a mud-colored, wintry landscape, and even its newest buildings managed to look old. Too many of the faces Keller saw around him on the street looked old too, even when they weren't, and gave weary evidence of lives wasted.

Cade was a haven of recreation for cowboys, buffalo hunters, freighters, and those who traveled the Brazos country with no real profession to attach to their names. It had more than its share of Indians too, mostly Tonkawas and Lipans. A group of the former were loitering on a nearby corner, passing around a bottle, gambling with a pair of dice, and hooting loudly at the outcome of each roll. Watching them with dark expressions were a few foot soldiers from Fort Cade, the stockaded enclosure that stood on the hill overlooking both the town and the wooded banks of Cade Creek, which flowed into the Brazos about two miles to the north.

The Brazos—in the older days called Brazos de Dios, the "Arms of God." Keller thought it very odd that such a seemingly vile town as Cade would lie in a country drained by a river with so grand and holy a name. Surely even the diety's arms weren't broad enough to embrace such a place as Cade.

He stopped long enough to roll a quirly, then continued down the street, trailing smoke behind him.

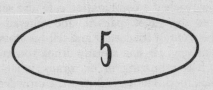

5

Being in Cade gave Keller the sense of a world apart from the rest of the nation—a nation at the moment distracted by its own approaching Centennial, the celebration of which many hoped would go far toward healing the rending wounds of a bloody war still too painfully fresh in the national memory. Keller had read in the newspapers about the big Centennial celebration up in Philadelphia and all the modern marvels it would display, and had realized that this was becoming quite an amazing world to live in. In the cities, people lighted their houses by lamps that were built right onto the wall and sent out gas jets for burning. There was talk about building suspended trains to carry people around big cities such as New York. At the same time, plans were taking shape for a canal to cut right across the Isthmus and make shipping from the east to west a far shorter and simpler affair. Keller had heard of something called a Corliss engine that supposedly ran itself with the power of a hundred horses times twenty-five . . . had heard of it, but didn't believe it, any more than he believed the even wilder story that a man in Boston had developed a machine that could send a man's voice through a wire to come out at the other end. Keller knew that wires could carry the pulses of telegraphs, but to carry an actual voice? That was too much for a born skeptic like Jed Keller to buy. Nobody was about to foist such foolishness on him!

Keller reached a combination café and saloon near the end of the street, paused, and entered when he caught the scent of fried meat and felt his stomach rumble responsively. He had already drunk too much whiskey and felt it buzzing in his brain; what he really needed was food. He walked past the crowded bar and headed for the collection of tables at the back. Sitting down, he ordered steak, biscuits, and coffee from an unshaven man who came to him with a blank pad and blanker expression. Then Keller sat back, rolled and lit another quirly, and eyed the crowd as he awaited his meal.

A man emerged from the crowd around the bar and made his way toward him, smiling pleasantly. Keller's eyes were drawn to him; he had the quick notion he knew this man from years past, but he could not place him. The fellow was dressed more fastidiously than anyone else in the place, though a closer look showed his clothes were thoroughly rumpled and dirty. Bringing his beer, the man came all the way to Keller's table, where he didn't wait for an invitation to sit down. He wordlessly scooted back the chair opposite Keller and flopped into it, his long legs sprawling out like those of a giant octopus Keller had once seen in an illustrated *Harper's Monthly* story about mysteries of the ocean.

"Hello, Jedford Keller," he said in a smooth voice. "My name is Lilly. Charles Lilly. Call me Charles, Charlie, Lilly, anything you wish, for that matter, as long as it doesn't besmirch my dear late mother."

Keller gave no answer, finding the man very odd. He was still struggling to figure out why he looked familiar.

"I hope you don't mind my intrusion into your evening," Lilly said.

Keller grunted noncommitally. He began to suspect Lilly was a gambler looking for an easy mark.

"Ah, but you're a silent man!" Lilly said. "Your sister was much the same way. Very little to say, most of the time."

Keller sat up straighter. Now Lilly had his attention. "You knew my sister?"

"Indeed I did. I was employed by her and Mr. Broadmore up until the tragedy."

Employed? Lilly certainly didn't look like a common ranch hand.

He apparently deciphered Keller's thoughts, for he chuckled and said, "I was the cook for the Broadmore ranch."

"I didn't think you looked like a cowboy. The truth is, you don't look like any ranch cook I've ever seen either."

Lilly took that as a compliment. "Why, thank you, sir. 'Praise above all—for praise prevails; heap up the measure, load the scales!' "

"What?"

"Pardon me, Mr. Keller. That was from Christopher Smart's 'A Song to David.' I often quote the great poets. It tends to annoy, I know, but it's an unbreakable habit."

Keller was thinking that Lilly was the strangest man he had ever met. He was elegant yet rumpled, scholarly yet earthy. Like a big-city schoolteacher who had been too long on holiday in the country.

"What do you want from me, Mr. Lilly?" Keller asked.

"Merely to make your acquaintance—and to offer my services to you in the cookhouse. It's my understanding you intend to operate the ranch."

"Where did you hear that?"

"From our mutual friend Till Cooke, earlier this morning."

Keller instantly felt less wary of Lilly. If he was a

friend of Cooke, he couldn't be a bad man. "To be honest, Mr. Lilly, I've not given any thought yet to hiring anyone in particular."

"You can't run a ranch that size alone—and if you'll allow me to make a suggestion, I believe you should give hastened effort to replenishing the ranch's staff of employees. Even as we speak, I'm certain Broadmore cattle are being quickly absorbed into other herds."

Keller's plate and cup arrived and were plunked down before him. The grubby waiter shuffled off, back to the bar. Keller began eating, figuring Lilly would leave. Instead, Lilly reached over, took one of the three biscuits on Keller's plate and began munching it.

"Excellent biscuits here," he said. "Except, of course, for the times you find weevils cooked in them. And they tend to be over-light on the salt and heavy on the lard."

Keller was more interested in other matters. "Is stock theft hereabouts as bad as everybody says it is?"

"Absolutely, sir. And Till Cooke, good man though he is, hasn't been able to affect it much. Not many fault him, though. The law sometimes lacks the teeth to take a big enough bite out of such things. It's one thing to arrest a horse thief and see him indicted. It's another entirely to see him remain for trial and go on through to conviction. Cooke is retiring to his ranch on good terms with the populace despite his failure to make much difference for them."

The silver-tongued Lilly dunked the usurped biscuit in his beer, took another bite, and chewed quite elegantly. At that moment the door opened and a sandy-haired man in spanking new clothes entered, limping slightly. There was an immediate reaction from those at the bar; their voices rose in simultaneous greeting. The newcomer grinned, waved at his greeters and then at everyone in general, and made his way to the bar. Following him was a stockier, flat-featured man, with brown hair that needed cutting.

"Give my friends here a fresh round of whatever they're drinking," he said in a loud voice. "And put it on my bill."

That prompted another jumble of happy exclamations as the sandy-haired man and his companion were engulfed by the already well-watered patrons.

Lilly had turned in his chair when the man came in. Turning back to Keller, he said, "Now, isn't that timely! There stands the very man who'll be taking on Till Cooke's off-cast mantle come election."

"Who is he?"

"David Ronald Weyburn. He's a local cattleman, and quite the popular man."

"Reckon he would be, buying drinks all around. Does he do that often?"

"He does. Particularly since he announced his candidacy for sheriff."

"Must be made out of money."

"He's got enough of it, and did even before he came to Cade. He now owns a ranch along Cade Creek north of town. He built himself a fine stone house, very large, though he lives alone in it except for a Mexican couple who tend house for him. He's a widower, I've heard."

"Who's that with him?"

"Floyd Fells. He lives in a little cabin on Weyburn's property, near the bunkhouse and stables and such, and runs much of the operation for Weyburn. The two come as a pair. Where you see Weyburn, you usually see Fells close behind."

"Who's running against Weyburn?"

"A drunken old soul named Jimmy Tripper. He hasn't a prayer of defeating the exalted Mr. Weyburn."

Keller remembered Till Cooke's negative comments about the man he anticipated would be the next sheriff.

He must have been referring to Weyburn. "So Weyburn's a sure bet, huh?"

"That's right . . . unless someone better soon emerges to challenge him. Which reminds me: Till Cooke tells me you are a man of the law. Perhaps you should consider—"

Keller cut him off. "Till hinted at the same. But no. Not me. From now on, I'm a cattleman, and that's all."

"Do you have experience with cattle ranching, Mr. Keller?"

"Not a lot," Keller admitted.

"All the more reason to move quickly to employ good men. I'll be glad to help you . . . if you will see fit to take me on."

By now Lilly had finished the stolen biscuit, so Keller grabbed the last one before it too could be taken. "I'll think on it," he said. In fact, he was already seriously considering the idea, for Lilly's talk about Broadmore stock being stolen concerned him. And Lilly, despite being an obvious eccentric, struck him favorably, especially given his friendship with Till Cooke. And Keller still had the notion he had met Lilly somewhere before.

Keller was surprised to notice that Weyburn had moved from the bar and was looking in his direction. When Weyburn lifted his glass in greeting, Keller nodded back, wondering why he had been singled out.

Lilly had noticed the exchange. "Does Weyburn know you?" he asked.

"Never met him," Keller said. "I guess he just figures I'm a vote he hasn't rounded up yet."

"It's probably that he knows who you are. Most around here do. It created a lot of interest when word got out that Magart Broadmore's own brother was in Cade."

Keller fell to his meal and finished it quickly. Standing, he prepared to go.

Lilly stood too. "About that job, Mr. Keller . . ."

Keller said, "I'll talk to Till. If he gives me good word on you, you're hired. Reckon I will need a cook, and someone who knows the locals enough to keep me from hiring scoundrels . . . aw, hang it all, just come on out to the ranch tomorrow. I'm moving out there in the morning. I'll be living in the bunkhouse to start out. I reckon if you don't turn out, I can always fire you."

"A man can ask no more than a fair shake. Thank you, sir. Until tomorrow."

"Right." Keller walked toward the door. As he left, he glanced back over his shoulder toward the bar. Weyburn was looking back at him, and once again lifted his glass.

Keller pretended not to have seen. As he walked onto the street, where the Tonkawas still hooted over their dice and the music of a saloon band made a tinny sound in the night, Keller noted that Weyburn's interest had made him feel unsettled, and he wasn't sure quite why.

He headed back to the Big Dakota, spent an hour halfheartedly reading an old newspaper somebody had dropped in the hall, then blew out the light and retired. A couple of hours after he fell asleep, he heard voices in the hallway outside the door. Two men, he judged from their sound. He grimaced when he heard the door of the room beside his open, then slam. Now they were inside, talking loudly, their voices coming through the wall. At least one of them was very drunk.

Keller began to fume and was about to pound the wall for silence when he heard the door open again. One of the men left, striding loudly down the hall and stairs. The firmness of the stride told Keller this was the sober one. Sure enough, the man left in the room began to sing, his voice slurred and atonal.

Keller hammered the wall with his fist. "Shut up in there!" he yelled.

"Sorry, friend," the drunk called back. "Mighty sorry. I'm drunk, that's all. Just drunk."

After that, Keller heard no more from the man.
Within a few minutes he was snoring peacefully, dream-
ing he was a child again and that he and Magart were
playing together on the muddy bank of the pond at the
old homeplace in Missouri.

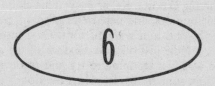

6

Keller's first thought the next morning was that he had been terribly foolish to hire a poetry-spouting stranger simply because he was interesting and insistent. Just who was Charlie Lilly, anyway? He claimed to know Till Cooke—but it was always possible he knew him only because Cooke had locked him up one time or another.

He'd just have to find out. Keller rose, washed, and after breakfasting in the restaurant that adjoined the Big Dakota, went straight to Till Cooke's office. He found his old friend coughing raggedly over a cup of coffee and a cigar—his usual "breakfast," Cooke explained.

Cooke, to Keller's pleasure, gave a good report on Lilly, confirming that he had indeed worked on the Broadmore ranch, and was considered by all a fine cook and reliable man, even if he was eccentric. Cooke then renewed his invitation for Keller to dine with him and his niece that night, and Keller again accepted, obtained directions, then headed back to the Big Dakota to check out.

He had lived at the hotel since coming to Cade, and was weary of it. Keller was no townsman by nature, despite all the years that his law enforcement duties had required him to live in or close to towns. As a rancher he would be free of that requirement; he looked forward to waking up without the bustle and clamor of streets and boardwalks right outside his window.

At the Big Dakota, Keller packed his clothing, gathered up his bundles, and departed the room, pulling the door shut behind him with his foot. Overburdened, he dropped a bundle just outside the door of the adjoining room. He was just stooping to try and retrieve it without dropping something else when the door opened.

"Give you a hand, friend?" a tired voice said.

"I'd be obliged," Keller replied. He stood, realizing at the same time that the man offering help had to be the drunk he had yelled at the night before. The man was crouching as Keller stood up—Keller noted the man's thin, sandy hair, tousled and spiked from sleep, and his rumpled clothing—and the man rose again, bundle in hand, and faced him.

It was David Weyburn. The two men looked at each other in obvious surprise.

Weyburn spoke first. "Mr. Keller, I believe?"

"That's right. How do you know me?"

"Word of your presence in Cade has made the rounds. I'm David Weyburn—I saw you last night at your meal. I'm very pleased to meet you. I was a friend, you see, of your late sister. And her husband too, of course. Please accept my condolences. Her passing was quite a tragedy."

"Yes. Thank you," Keller said.

"She thought highly of you, you know."

No, Keller didn't know, though he was glad to hear it now. At the time she died, Magart was still cut off from her family; Keller had assumed his sister harbored ill will toward him because of that.

"You look surprised, Mr. Keller, but what I say is true," Weyburn said. His voice sounded weary, and his face bore witness to a headache so bad that Keller could almost feel it himself. "I should tell you that I was aware of the division in your family. Magart . . . Mrs. Broadmore, I mean, talked about it pretty openly with her close friends. She had nothing but good, however, to say about you. She would have been happy to know you had come looking for her."

"Beg pardon, Mr. Weyburn, but how is it you know that's why I came here?"

Weyburn smiled. "Why else would you have come? Anyway, everybody in Cade tends to know everybody else's business. Or so they think. Folks here like to talk, and you've been quite a source of interest. Your little foray with Paco the Mex heated up the gossip something fierce."

Keller was amazed and offended that a man he had just met would bring up such a touchy subject. He was further offended when Weyburn took the issue a step farther.

"Let me ask you, Mr. Keller—why did you attack the Mexican?"

Keller gave Weyburn a look that should have sent him wilting back. But Weyburn continued to look him in the eye. Keller realized how very badly Weyburn wanted to know the answer.

"My business with Paco was private," Keller replied. "Why do you think it's yours?"

Weyburn shifted uncomfortably on his feet. "I heard that Paco might have been spreading false stories about me. He does that. Tells lies about people. You can't believe what he says."

"I've heard."

"He didn't say anything to you about me . . . did he?"

This conversation was becoming altogether too bizarre. Keller could have laughed in disbelief.

"He didn't say a word about anyone or anything— though frankly, Mr. Weyburn, I don't think I'd be obliged to tell you if he had. Now, if you'll be so kind as to stuff that bundle under my arm here . . ."

Weyburn did. He didn't seem offended by Keller's gruff speech; if anything, he appeared relieved. "I would offer to carry some of that downstairs for you, Mr. Keller, but I'm not fit for a public appearance right now. I'm running for sheriff, you see, and last night I drank a little too much while out stirring votes. I came up here to sleep it off instead of going home drunk."

Keller wasn't interested. He clamped the bundle between his elbow and side. "Good-bye, Mr. Weyburn."

"Good day, Mr. Keller."

Keller made it down the stairs without dropping anything else. Weyburn, a thoughtful expression on his face, turned and reentered his room, and as he walked, he limped. On his leg was a shallow bullet wound that had been healing, but which he had somehow managed to tear partly open again while he was drunk.

Keller was on his way to the Broadmore ranch before it hit him that what Weyburn had said could be construed as establishing a chilling connection between Weyburn and Magart's death. Keller had been told that Paco knew something secret about the fire at the Broadmore ranch. Weyburn, on the other hand, had said that Paco's alleged secret information supposedly involved him. Two distinct notions—unless really they weren't distinct at all. Could Paco's secret have linked Weyburn to the fire in some way?

Keller thought about that as he rode toward the Broadmore ranch. A friend of Magart's, he claimed to have been. Keller hadn't failed to notice the way Weyburn had spoken primarily of Magart, adding in Folly Broadmore as if in afterthought. He wasn't sure what it all meant, if anything. He grew tired of thinking about it.

Keller reached the ranch and was actually disappointed to find that Lilly was not awaiting him. Had the man backed out of the job he had asked for? Now that

Keller had reason to believe Lilly a sound fellow, he didn't want to lose him.

As the mounting sun warmed the morning air and drew from the land moist, organic scents that hinted of the coming spring, Keller opened up the bunkhouse shutters and doors, letting the breeze blow through and the sunshine spill in. He found an old broom and swept out the filth, sending big dust clouds into the air. He was just finishing when he saw Lilly riding in.

"Good morning to you, Mr. Keller!" Lilly brightly proclaimed as he dismounted.

"It's almost noon, in case you hadn't noticed," Keller replied.

"So it is!" Lilly replied. "If I had run any later, you surely would have thought the worst of me." He led his horse to the stable and returned, loading a pipe. " 'Tobacco, tobacco, sing sweetly for tobacco! Tobacco is like love, oh love it!' " he boomed out, then grinned. "Tobias Hume, poet. Not to be confused with David Hume, philosopher."

Keller grinned back, privately wondering how such an eccentric as Lilly had managed to hold his own among the rough-hewn personnel of a Texas ranch, for whom "poetry" meant either sentimental, sugary verse about mother back home or perhaps ribald doggerel scribbled on the wall of some sporting house privy.

Keller told Lilly that based on Till Cooke's good word about him, he wanted Lilly not only to be ranch cook, but also to help him hire other ranch personnel. In fact, Lilly would have chief authority on the matter, for Keller realized he was new here, and also knew his own inherent limitations. He was no cattleman, not yet. He was a good judge of men as men, but not necessarily of men as cowboys.

Lilly was obviously pleased by the confidence being invested him. "I will hire you the finest hands available east of the Llano Estacado," he vowed.

They worked hard the rest of the day, repairing and cleaning the bunkhouse, which was substantially run-down, and readying the cookhouse for use again. Lilly was obviously in his element in the cookhouse, and for the first time Keller was able to perceive him as a cook. Despite Lilly's poetry and faded elegance, he looked perfectly in place amid the pots, pans, and kettles, all of which had escaped theft during the period after the fire.

Keller could only hope his stock out there in the rolling cattle country had fared as well as the cookhouse dishes. He was eager to investigate just how badly the cattle thieves of the Brazos had hurt him. He didn't feel optimistic.

That evening, Keller paid the expected visit to Till Cooke and his niece. Cooke had been right: Claire O'Keefe was certainly not the skinny child Jed Keller had known. She was as tall as her gangly girlhood had promised she would be, but beyond that, all childhood indicators of her physical destiny had proven deceptive. Gone was the freckle-faced, gap-toothed, clumsy girl. Claire O'Keefe was now a shapely, poised beauty with hair the color of honey and a smile that could warm a room. Keller sat in the front room of Cooke's log ranch house, coffee cup in hand, and wondered how any man could have been fool enough to divorce a woman such as Claire.

"This place shows the feminine touch real nice," Keller said, looking around the room.

"Claire's done a lot to brighten these four walls," Cooke replied. "You should have seen it before she came."

Claire cast up her eyes at the memory. "I wasn't sure if I had found the house or stumbled into a pig-pen," she said.

"Ouch!" Cooke said, laughing. "Now, Claire, it wasn't that bad, was it?"

"I don't see how Aunt Carolina put up with a man

possessing habits like yours," Claire replied. Despite her forthrightness, Keller could detect her affection for her uncle.

"I wasn't like this when Carolina was still with me," Cooke said. "She wouldn't allow it."

"Carolina was a fine woman," Keller said. "I never figured how you managed to talk her into marrying you, Till."

"You know, Jed, I never figured that out either," he said, and for a moment there was a palpable dip in the levity; Cooke's eyes became misty, and he quickly turned his head. At that point Claire turned to Keller and declared brightly that if he didn't have another piece of cake she'd feel insulted.

"Make it a big one, then," he replied. And when she was gone off to fetch it, he sat admiring the way she had interjected herself to save her uncle embarrassment as his emotion for his lost wife broke through. Till Cooke had never been the kind who was comfortable showing his feelings before others. Even at Carolina Cooke's funeral, Cooke had staunchly refused to let himself be seen shedding tears.

Conversation for the rest of the evening ranged all around the various aspects of the Texas ranching business, of "Texas fever" and cattle prices, railroads and range lands, and inevitably, rustlers. Once again Keller was struck with the fatalistic attitude Cooke had toward stock theft along the Brazos. "I've been unable to stop it in all my time in office," he said. "I'm convinced there's some things that can't be dealt with from the backside of a badge."

Keller wasn't sure what Cooke meant by that, but didn't inquire. He was far too distracted by Claire O'Keefe to think deeply about much else.

When he left an hour later and rode toward his own spread, he found he could recall only a little of what Cooke had talked about, but every word, gesture, and movement of Claire's was firmly ensconced in his memory.

She had asked him to come back and visit again, whenever he could. "I will," he had told her. And he had meant it.

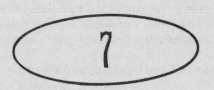

7

The next few weeks were filled with constant activity; Keller went through a paradoxical time of learning that he was anything in the world but a real Texas cattleman, while becoming more a cattleman every day. The work was harder than he had expected, but he liked it. It was healing and even pleasant at times. The only deeply aggravating part was that it kept him too busy to visit Claire O'Keefe as often as he would have liked.

His friendship with Charlie Lilly, meanwhile, had grown strong. Lilly was as good as his promise, and hired Keller a small but capable group of hands, some of whom had worked for Folly Broadmore and thus felt at home back on the familiar ranch. To a man, they treated Keller with great respect, despite his inexperience, and in time he discovered this was due to the fact that he was Magart Broadmore's brother. Magart, he found, had been revered by her husband's men. *She was a good woman,* they would say when they talked of her. *Too good a woman for Folly Broadmore.*

Two things clouded Keller's experience in rebuilding the ranch. One was the way the place kept putting him in mind of Magart; whenever he crossed the rise beyond the bunkhouse, his eyes were drawn to the two graves and the charred rubble of the Broadmore house. At last he put two of his men to work hauling the burned timbers to a nearby draw, where they burned what wood remained. And, unknown to Keller, Lilly told the men to be careful not to talk much of Magart Broadmore in Keller's presence. He had noted the way Keller's features drew tight and grim when the subject came up.

The second and bigger cloud for Keller was the discovery that, as feared, much of the ranch's stock had simply vanished. Too few of the cattle he and his men found on the hills and in the gullies for miles around the ranch bore the Broadmore brand.

"It's the thieving Wyeths," said Doyle Boston, perhaps the best of the cowboys Lilly had hired. "I'd like to stretch my rope with them Wyeths, that's for damn sure."

Keller didn't have to be told who the Wyeths were. As far away as Missouri, the Wyeths—a loosely knit gaggle of lowlifes whose name came from that of their recognized leader, Roy "Cutter" Wyeth—were cattle thieves who ranged up and down the Brazos and as far north as Dodge. Occasional forays by Texas Rangers, special posses, and soldiers out of Fort Cade had weakened the gang periodically, but had never wiped it out. Hydralike, it seemed to grow new tentacles each time one was cut off.

Not all Keller's men shared Boston's conviction about the Wyeths. Cutter Wyeth, they said, supposedly spent most of his time in Kansas now. They said that Boston tended to see the Wyeth hand in every cattle theft that happened, when in fact there were plenty of supposedly legitimate cattlemen who weren't averse to cutting into their neighbors' herds if a good opportunity came—and the death of the Broadmores had certainly been that.

Keller didn't know who to believe, and it hardly mattered. What mattered was that his herd was diminished, and his profitability would be diminished accordingly. Keller was beginning to understand why Till Cooke had been so discouraging about his plans to become a rancher.

Spring came to the Brazos country and painted the rolling terrain with a beauty that Jed Keller found awesome.

On the grounds of the Broadmore ranch—for it popularly retained that name despite Keller's ownership—daisies probed up from the greening land, moving in the breeze so their yellow and white blossoms looked like the bobbing heads of a fancily arrayed army. Texas filaree, dalea, clammyweed, and larkspur added their own touches of lavender, pink, yellow, white, and purple to the landscape. For a few brief days the pricklypear opened its big yellow-orange blossoms; these brought exclamations of delight from Charlie Lilly, who anticipated making jelly from the cactus fruit that would follow.

Once, when no one was about to see him, Keller picked a huge bouquet of wildflowers and rode all the way to the Cooke ranch to present them to Claire. It was the clearest indicator he had given of the way he was beginning to feel about her, and she pleased him by praising the flowers as if they were the rarest of beauties, even though identical ones grew all around her own residence, and bouquets like the one Keller had brought already decorated her table and mantelpiece.

Keller rode home with a grin on his face, thinking how much he loved the springtime and how benevolent the Creator had been to make womenfolk, especially womenfolk like Claire O'Keefe.

The landscape now looked lovelier than ever to Jed Keller. The best part of it, he decided, were the trees—for on a Texas landscape, trees were things that stood out to be noticed. Along the streams, pecan trees put out their leaves, and the thorny chittam shrubs grew thicker and stronger. Also welcoming spring along the waterways were elms, willows, soapberries, and an assortment of ivies that twined around and up them. On the hills and in the gullies, the white shinoak, buckeye, and elbow bushes had shaken off the winter and turned hardy again. Sumac sent out its distinctive scent, and the mesquite trees in particular were objects of delight for the transplanted Missourian.

Some days later, even the usually ugly town of Cade looked like it had put on new clothes, for gaudy banners stretched across the street and ribbon-tied garlands hung on doors and in windows. The special election had come and gone, and as had been widely expected, David Weyburn had easily taken the sheriff's post, his abundant votes bought substantially by his generosity at the local saloons. That generosity remained intact; the great victory celebration in Cade was being held at Weyburn's expense.

As evening fell on the celebration, Cade was even more crowded than usual, for the ranches and sodbuster spreads had all but emptied. Cade had plenty of festivity to offer at any time, but it usually wasn't free, so no one wanted to miss this opportunity. Jed Keller walked slowly down the decorated street, Till Cooke at his side, and watched the mounting celebration.

Till Cooke and Jed Keller were two of four men in town not in a very festive mood, though Cooke was pretending hard to be. Keller sensed that with Cooke's relinquishment of his post close at hand, the old lawman was feeling a little maudlin. Keller himself was dejected simply because Claire was not here; she was under the weather and had foregone the celebration. The other two noncelebrants were Homer and Haman Polk, both already informed by Weyburn that their employment would not continue. Their careers in law enforcement had died embryonic deaths.

"Look at him up there," Cooke said, gesturing at Weyburn, who was all smiles and handshakes on the reception platform built in front of the Big Dakota. Behind him Floyd Fells, atypically dressed up, was tugging at his stiff celluloid collar and fidgeting like a bad boy in church. "I reckon Weyburn figures Cade is all his now. And I suppose it is, in one way of looking at it. I just hope this county likes its new keeper as much as it thinks it will."

"You never have told me why it is you don't trust Weyburn," Keller said.

Cooke smiled without humor. "Instinct, Jed, instinct. And a few rumors, the really quiet kind that mean more than the loud ones."

Keller thought about Weyburn's talk of "lies" supposedly told about him by Paco the Mex, and wondered if these were the same rumors Cooke referred to. He had never told Cooke of his strange encounter with Weyburn in the Big Dakota. "What rumors?" he asked.

"That David Weyburn might not be the fine and honest rancher he puts himself up to be. There's a few who think he might have reached into his neighbors herds a few times when nobody was looking."

"You don't say?" Keller looked at Weyburn with new interest.

"No, I don't say . . . but some do. I even have to wonder, Jed, if you might not find some Broadmore stock mixed in with his herd, if you cared to look."

Keller frowned at that, and took a sip from the free beer he had picked up at one of the laden tables near Weyburn's stand. Weyburn—taking Broadmore cattle? Perhaps that, and not the Broadmore ranch fire, explained Weyburn's curiosity about him, and about the "lies" Paco supposedly had been spreading.

"Till, if Weyburn's a stock thief, then having him in as sheriff is going to make things hellacious for the ranchers. Not that it ain't hellacious enough already. I ain't heard of a cattleman within a hundred miles of Cade who hasn't lost stock this year. Cattle and horses both."

"I know of one," Cooke replied. "He's standing up on that platform with a new suit and a big 'possum grin on his face."

"Weyburn's not lost any stock?"

"Not that I've heard of."

"Maybe he's just been lucky."

"Maybe he makes his own luck."

"Till, you're a suspicious soul."

"I am indeed, when it comes to Weyburn." Cooke turned to face Keller directly. He paused for a moment before saying anything more, and when he spoke, his voice was quieter, more serious. "You know, Jed, when you have to enforce the law but stay within the law yourself, there's only so much you can do. The law's a funny thing: Maybe sometimes you have to break it just a little to put a halt to somebody else breaking it a lot worse."

There, again—another cryptic commentary from Till Cooke on lawbreaking. This time Keller didn't let it pass. "What's that kind of talk supposed to mean?" he asked.

Cooke hesitated, as if he had said too much. "Likely things will come clear soon enough, if it goes that far." He gave a fraternal punch to Keller's shoulder. "See you later. I'm going after some of that beer."

"See you later, Till."

Walking alone, Keller wondered what Cooke had been getting at. He also wondered if Cooke's suspicions about Weyburn had any meat, or if they were just the way the old lawman was expressing that inevitable tinge of jealousy toward the man who had taken his old job. Even though Cooke had stepped down voluntarily, Keller figured he had to feel slightly resentful of Weyburn, whom the public was greeting with such enthusiasm.

Keller meandered through the crowd, greeting those he knew, but keeping to himself. As of yet he didn't feel completely at home in Cade, though he did at the ranch itself. He no longer lived in the bunkhouse; he had built a small ranch house. It was still temporarily roofed with canvas, but he liked it.

"Please, please, no more . . ."

He had wandered beyond the fringe of the crowd, and heard the pleading voice from a nearby alley. Following the plea came the sounds of grunts and thuds. A man was being beaten back in that alley. Keller had no idea who, or why—but it wasn't his way to stand by while another human being was brutalized.

He darted into the alley, drawing his pistol, and came around the back of the building. He found two toughs pounding mercilessly on a third man. Keller swung back his pistol, clouted the closer of the antagonists in the side of the skull, then shoved the other to the earth with the bottom of his foot.

He saw then that the victim was Paco the Mex.

8

Paco reached up and began babbling gratefully until he saw who his rescuer was. He screeched and covered his face with crossed forearms, probably assuming that Keller had knocked the other two away in order to get his own chance at him.

Keller had no time to give reassurances, for both toughs were now up and coming at him, too mad and drunk to consider that he held a drawn pistol and they had no weapons but their fists.

Keller waited until the closer one got within striking distance, then ducked the man's wild punch. At the same time, Keller came straight up with the pistol barrel and laid open the man's chin with the sight. Groping for his split chin, the man buckled to his knees; Keller used his own knee to flatten the man's nose and lay him out on his back, his calves doubling up under his thighs.

The second man pulled up short at the last instant, seeing what had happened to his partner. Keller lifted the pistol and aimed it directly between the man's eyes; the man waved his hands, wet his pants, staggered backward, then turned and ran. The downed man stumbled to his feet and followed, dripping blood between his fingers from his tightly gripped chin.

Keller took a deep breath and holstered his pistol. Looking down at Paco, he saw a face livid with fright.

"Don't fret, Paco," he said. "You don't have anything more to fear from me. I was drunk when I attacked you, and I'd been told you knew things." He reached down to help Paco stand. "I hope you'll accept my apology."

Paco looked like he might faint, perhaps from the trauma of the attack, or from surprise at being apologized to by a man who had previously threatened his life. Almost as drunk as the men who had attacked him, Paco stood on his one real foot and one wooden peg, wobbled a bit, and then leaned back against the wall.

"Gracias, Señor Keller," he said. "You are a good man, a very good man."

"Why'd those two jump you?"

"They thought I had money, señor. They thought I had stolen money from a saloon."

"Had you?"

"Oh, no, no—I am no thief."

Keller glanced down and saw several bills sticking out of Paco's pockets, but saw no reason to say anything about them. "You seem to have come through all right, Paco. You'd best steer clear of that pair, though."

"Si, *Señor* Keller. I will."

Keller walked back toward the street, then turned again when Paco came after him, calling his name.

"What?" Keller asked.

"*Señor* . . ." Paco paused, licking his lips nervously. "*Señor* . . . about your sister . . . she . . ." He paused, licking his lips nervously. "Your sister . . . it is not like the people all say, about the fire—" He cut off abruptly, his eyes flickering to the left as he seemingly looked past Keller. Despite his swarthy complexion, he visibly blanched. "No, no. I can say nothing. . . . I have told you nothing, nothing!"

He turned and stumped away, grunting each time he lifted the peg leg.

"Paco!" Keller bellowed, heading after him. "Paco, come here and talk to me!"

Paco would not turn; he moved away more swiftly than ever. Keller reached him and grasped his shoulder, wheeling him around so swiftly that the Mexican almost fell.

"Tell me what you were going to say, Paco!"

"Señor, please . . . I am a dead man already! In the alley . . ."

Keller looked behind him. At the head of the alley stood Floyd Fells. Fells, who by now had yanked away his aggravating celluloid collar, was looking right at Paco with a harsh expression. His eyes flickered to Keller but did not stay on him. Fells was within easy earshot and had surely heard what Paco had been saying. Keller realized the sight of Fells must have been what made Paco blanche.

"I am dead! Dead!" Paco said despairingly. He wrenched free of Keller's grasp and stumped off in the opposite direction.

Keller watched him go and did not follow. When he turned back toward the street, Fells was gone.

David Weyburn rode home alone from the celebration, for despite his public sociability, he also required much privacy. He needed solitude in order to think clearly, to separate the public Weyburn from the private one—the real one, the one few ever came to know.

Weyburn had built his big stone house two rolling hills away from the bunkhouse, corral, and other buildings of the ranch that Floyd Fells operated on his behalf. The house was uncommonly large for its few occupants; common speculation in Cade was that Weyburn was hopeful of marrying and raising a big family someday, and had optimistically built his house to accommodate lots of youngsters. It was as good an explanation as any, and Weyburn let it stand.

He had left the celebration back in town running full tilt, as it probably would all night. With any luck, nobody would get drunk enough to spark a shooting or stabbing, especially if the Tonkawas could be kept away from the beer. Even if there was trouble, it wasn't yet Weyburn's worry, with Till Cooke still officially the sheriff for some time yet.

Though it was very dark, Weyburn's horse had learned the route back to the ranch and plodded along with no need of guidance. Weyburn slumped in the saddle and let himself relax; it had been a busy day, and he had smiled so much his jaws ached. He all but fell asleep in the saddle, but this was no accident; he had taught himself to achieve this state of near-slumber without descending deeper into full sleep, and by this means he regularly renewed his energy so efficiently that he sometimes slept only four hours at night and felt none the worse for it the next morning.

At his gate he lifted his head—and abruptly pulled his horse to a halt. A light burned downstairs, in his office, but no lamps had been lit when he left the house. Glancing up, he saw that the light was out in the upstairs bedroom of his servants, Eduardo and Maria Cruz; at this hour, they were almost certainly asleep. He dismounted, tethered his horse to the gate, drew his pistol and advanced stealthily toward the window. Probably Eduardo or Maria had entered the room for some reason and carelessly failed to extinguish the lamp, but Weyburn could take no chances.

Weyburn crouched at the base of the window. He was glad for his caution, because he heard footfalls on the floor inside. Someone was pacing back and forth in his office. Then came the clink of glass on glass, and Weyburn knew that whoever it was had gotten into his private stock of whiskey. Carefully he lifted his head and looked in. Then he swore aloud, stood, and rapped on the window with the butt of his pistol. The man inside was ratty-bearded, almost lipless, and possessed a badly drooping right eye. He dropped his just-refreshed shot glass, swung into a half crouch, whipped out his pistol and leveled it on the face peering back at him from the outside.

"Weyburn!" he declared, the drooping right eye twitching a little, as it did when he was startled or nervous. "Hell, I almost shot you!"

Weyburn fired the man an angry look, then headed around the house to the front door. Entering, he met the man in the door of his office and jammed a finger into his face. "Cutter Wyeth, what the hell do you think you're doing, coming into my house with me away? You trying to ruin both of us? What if somebody saw you?"

"Nobody saw me, Weyburn. You know I'm careful." Wyeth grinned. His way of grinning, Weyburn had noticed long ago, only made him uglier.

"Where are Eduardo and Maria?"

"Upstairs asleep. Eduardo let me in and said I could wait for you here."

Weyburn pushed Wyeth back inside his office and closed the door. Moving with the swiftness of a man much perturbed, he went to each window and drew the heavy curtains, then lit a couple more lamps to brighten the room. Wyeth, meanwhile, refilled his shot glass and watched Weyburn with a vaguely haughty expression.

"Next drink you get, get it from the bottle under the bar," Weyburn instructed tersely. "That one you're pulling on cost me far too much to be wasted on as rough a palate as yours."

Wyeth didn't know what a palate was, and Weyburn could tell the old thief was trying to figure out if he had been insulted. That struck Weyburn as funny and took the edge off his anger. He sighed and waved in resignation. "Cutter, drink out of whichever bottle you want," he said. "You and I will be making enough money over the next few years to buy plenty of fine whiskey."

Cutter Wyeth smiled. "Them's musical words to my ears, Sheriff. Musical words." He lifted the glass and drained it in a swallow.

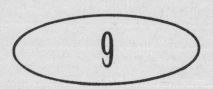

9

Weyburn went to the liquor cabinet and poured himself a shot. "I didn't expect to see you back so soon, Cutter. My wire said there was no cause to rush. The main thing was just to let you know I had won the race, and that we should be in for high cotton."

"I had to get away from Dodge anyhow," Wyeth said. "Things were getting too hot for me there." He licked the rim of his glass with a tongue that made Weyburn recall an eternally drooling beagle he had owned as a boy. "I had trouble over a woman, and shot a fellow. Didn't kill him. Just shot him, that's all. I should've killed him, though, because damned if that woman didn't turn around and take him in to nurse him back healthy again. It was all for nothing."

Weyburn had to wonder why any woman willing to associate with a maggot like Cutter Wyeth could possibly be worth shooting anyone over. The thought prudently remained private.

"Any men with you?"

"A few. They're in the old line cabins over on the Clear Fork right now. I come here to your place alone. Nobody saw me but Eduardo."

"Good. Always come alone—and only at night."

He took a small sip of his drink. "Actually, you've picked a good time to show up, Cutter. There's some cattle I want you to steal."

"Whose?"

"Mine."

"Yours?"

"That's right. I want you to steal some of my cattle. Maybe fifteen, twenty head."

"What for?"

"To avert suspicion. You think others haven't already noticed that my herd doesn't suffer like the rest? I've heard a few suspicious whispers I don't like."

"Hell, there can't be much suspicion. You got elected, didn't you?"

"There's plenty of votes for sale in Cade for the price of a few glasses of beer, and besides, I didn't have any real competition. We can't get overconfident and reckless, Cutter, or they'll be on us like a cheap suit on an undertaker. I've already heard a mention or two of the Old Boys going to work again. We sure as hell don't need that."

Wyeth walked over to an expensive stuffed chair and flopped down. Weyburn eyed the outlaw's greasy clothing and wondered how much essence of Wyeth would remain smeared on the chair when the man got up again.

"You've got you a real nice place here, Weyburn. I sure would like to have a place like this. I'd be happy just to sleep in one of them big feather beds of yours sometime."

Weyburn said nothing. When it became clear no further hospitality was forthcoming, Wyeth sighed, stretched, and stood. "I'll be going now."

"That's probably a good idea," Weyburn said.

"I'll bet I know why you want me out." Wyeth put on an odd grin.

"What do you mean?"

"I heard a woman's voice upstairs. You got you a sweet thing waiting for you up there, partner?"

Weyburn wore no smile. "You heard Maria. That's the only woman in this house."

"Didn't sound like Maria."

"It was. Now shut up and get on out of here. Be careful you're not seen riding out."

Wyeth said, "You need to talk friendlier to me, Weyburn. I don't like being talked down to. It makes me mad . . . and you don't want me mad."

"Accept my apology, then. Just get on with you—it's dangerous for you to be here."

"You fret too much, Weyburn. You always have. Good evening to you." Wyeth rolled his eyes toward the ceiling. "Yours is bound to be better than mine."

When Wyeth was gone, Weyburn went outside, fetched his horse where he had left it at the gate, and stabled it for the night. Returning to the house, he lit a lamp and walked up the dark stairs with it. He passed his servants' door; Eduardo was snoring loudly, with Maria doing her best to top his volume. He continued down the hall to his own room.

Lowering the flame of the lamp, he entered. The dim light fell on the wheelchair parked just inside the doorway. He walked to the bed.

The woman there awakened slowly, then smiled up at him.

"Hello, my dear," he said.

"David, you're here." Her hands rose toward him. "I'm glad you're here." In her voice was a quality that set it apart from other women's voices. A softness, a childishness of tone.

Weyburn didn't mind it. This was the woman he loved, the woman who was both his greatest possession and greatest risk. He set the lamp on the table by the bed and lowered himself into her embrace.

*   *   *

Weyburn was eating a solitary breakfast the next morning when the knocker on his door hammered three times. Both Eduardo and Maria were out, clearing the garden patch that would soon be planted with vegetables. Weyburn rose, wiped his mouth on a checkered napkin, and went to the door.

"Oh, it's you, Floyd. Come in."

"Got any coffee, David?"

"On the stove. Help yourself."

Floyd Fells moved familiarly through the house to the kitchen, and came back a few moments later with a steaming cup and a hunk of bread torn off one of Weyburn's loaves. Floyd seated himself at Weyburn's table and came straight to the point. "I saw something in town last night that may mean trouble for us."

Weyburn sighed. Fells was always smelling trouble. "Go on."

"I was meandering around in the celebration, you know, and I came to the end of an alley and saw Paco the Mex talking to that Keller fellow. Magart's brother."

Weyburn began to grow concerned. "Yes. I met him."

"Paco was about to tell him something . . . something about the fire—that much I picked up. And Paco looked scared half to death when he saw me. Turned and ran."

Weyburn had gone white. He swore. "So he *does* know! But how could he? It's impossible! We covered ourselves so well. . . ." He stood, overturning his coffee cup and ignoring it. "Do you think he told Keller?"

"No, but he came close. If he hadn't seen me when he did, he would have spilled it all."

Weyburn paced about, rubbing his chin. "So what are we going to do about it, then?"

"Only one answer I can think of."

It took a couple of seconds for Weyburn to understand Fells's implication. "No!" he declared. "No more killing. There's been enough of that already."

"Look, David, I don't like it any more than you do. But what's been done up until now has been necessary, and now it's necessary again. We can't let it fall apart now."

"I don't like it. I don't like it at all."

"You'd not like a hangman's noose or a jail cell any better."

Weyburn had nothing to say. He paced about. Fells sipped his coffee for a while, letting his employer get used to the unwelcome idea he had just been handed.

Weyburn slowly seemed to wilt. He sat down heavily. "You'll take care of it, Floyd?"

"So you agree it has to be done?"

Weyburn closed his eyes and took a deep breath. "I agree."

"That's good, because it's done already. I took care of Paco last night. I sliced his throat from ear to ear."

Weyburn looked like he might be sick.

"God, what a sorry business this is! What about the body?"

"Sunk in the Brazos."

"What if he's found?"

"He won't be. And if he is, there's nothing to link him to us. And anyway, the next sheriff won't likely find a single clue about his disappearance—will he?"

Weyburn smiled wanly. "No, he won't. That much, at least, we can be sure of." Then he sat silent awhile with his head in his hands. He looked up sharply. "Floyd, were you able to find out where Paco learned about what happened?"

"No. He fainted away on me when I grabbed him. I just made sure he didn't wake up. So I'm not sure just how much he really knew. Maybe almost nothing . . . not that we could take that chance."

"How could he have known anything at all? That's what I can't figure."

"Most likely he seen it. Think about it, David. You know how Magart always was free with the handouts. And old Paco had been around the Broadmore ranch that day—I seen him myself, walking away from the house with a loaf of Magart's bread, when we rode up. I figure that instead of going all the way back to town, he sat down out there in the grass to eat his bread. He would have been able to see it all—and we never knew he was there."

Weyburn stood up and paced around again, swearing beneath his breath and running his right hand repeatedly through his hair. "Three dead now," he said. "They'll hang us for certain, if it gets out!"

"It won't get out . . . unless your secret upstairs ends up making her presence known."

Weyburn aimed a stiff finger right at Fells. "You're starting to tread on thin ice, Floyd! You keep her out of this!"

"She's dangerous to us, David. I know you don't like to hear that, but it's true. Some things you can keep secret forever. A living and breathing woman you can't."

"She's my problem, not yours."

"You don't think so? Remember, it's my neck on the block too, David. It was me who killed the Tonkawa woman, and now Paco."

Weyburn was in no mood for further talk. Nor, for that matter, was Fells. He departed without another word passing between them.

Alone, Weyburn sighed loudly, ran his hand through his hair again, and headed to his office, where he downed a shot of whiskey, early though the hour was. He had planned to go into town today, but that idea had already been dropped. He was far too shaken to venture out in public.

He sat down and struggled to regain his composure. Finally, when his hands stopped shaking, he walked upstairs.

She was dressed now, awaiting him in her wheel-chair. A tray with the scraps of her breakfast, brought up by Maria before the day's gardening began, sat on the table.

"David," she said, "is it warm outside? I'd like to go out today."

"It's too cool, my dear."

"But Maria and Eduardo are working outside! It can't be very cold. Please, let me go out! I can't stay locked up in here forever!"

"Hush, dear, hush. You need to stay inside today. Try to walk a little if you can."

She looked disappointed. Weyburn was struck, as he often was, by what an odd creature this lady was. Her body was that of a woman, but all else about her was childlike. Inwardly he cursed the man whose violence had made her this way, the man he had made pay for that violence to the fullest extent.

"Will you be here with me today?" she asked.

Weyburn smiled. "Yes. Today I stay home. Today we're together, just the two of us."

Her face became animated with happiness. "Come and hug me, David," she said. "I love you so."

He went to her and put his arms around her. "And I love you too, my dear Magart. I love you more than anything else in this world."

She squeezed him so hard it drove the breath from him. He made no protest. Magart Broadmore was his, bought at the cost of murder and deceit, and his devotion to her was one of the few things in his life that wasn't pretense or fraud.

10

A Few Days Later

Jed Keller pulled the wagon to a halt in front of Till Cooke's office and threw on the brake. Dismounting, he tossed aside his tenth quirly of the day and walked up to the door. Through the pane he saw Cooke inside, pouring himself a cup of black coffee from the rusted pot on the stove. The door opened with a jangle and Cooke looked up.

"Well, hello there, Jed. How you been?"

"Fine, Till. How's yourself?"

"Tolerably well, all things considered."

"And how's Claire?"

"Talking about you every minute. That woman's affections are set for you, Keller. You'd best watch out, or she'll catch you."

Keller grinned. "I'm done caught, Till."

"I know it. I'd have to be blind to miss it."

The sheriff sat down on the corner of his battered desk and shook his head. Around the office were various crates laden with personal items that through his years in office had found their home in his office, and which now had to be moved out to make way for Weyburn.

"Looks like you've been busy here, Till."

"Yes indeed. And not just with packing up. It's been right odd. Jed, in all my time in this office I've never had anybody come in and report a missing person, and since I talked to you last, I've had two."

"That is peculiar. Hey, can I have some of that coffee?"

"Help yourself—you can use Haman's cup there, if it's clean enough to suit. The first one in was a Tonkawa they call Rooster Jack; he came in the day after Weyburn's big celebration and told me his wife has been missing for several weeks. I asked him why the devil he waited so long to report it, and he said she's took off on him before, but she's always come back. This time she hasn't. Lordy, it took me ten minutes to get him to even tell me her name!"

Keller was swabbing out Haman's rather crusty cup with his shirttail. "Why?"

"Tonkawas don't believe in saying the names of the dead. Bad medicine. They won't even give the name of a dead person to a baby—that's why they got such loco names sometimes. They run out of the usual ones, you see, and start borrowing from the Comanches and the white folks. Claire's danged scared of the Tonkawas, by the way. She can't get comfortable about folks who've occasionally been known to eat the flesh of their dead enemies."

"I'd heard something about that, I think. So this Rooster Jack believes his wife is dead, then?"

"He's beginning to think so. But I finally got out of him that her name's Winnie. If you hear anything about her, tell me . . . at least until my term is up—Lord hasten the day."

Keller took a careful sip of steaming coffee. It was as black as tar and almost as thick, but he liked it that way. "Who's the second missing party?"

"None other than your old friend Paco the Mex."

Keller's cup stopped in mid-lift. "Paco? How long's he been gone?"

"Since the night of Weyburn's victory celebration."

Keller swore.

"What is it?" Cooke asked.

"I talked to Paco that night—after I helped beat off two roughnecks trying to take his money."

"Lordy! You reckon they might have done away with him later?"

"It's possible—of course, if you want to suspect everybody who has tousled with old Paco, you'd have to include me."

"No. I know you, Jed. You're no murderer. But I want to hear about them other two."

Keller told what he could, but the truth was he hadn't known either man, and hadn't paid much attention to their faces.

What really caught Cooke's attention was Keller's mention of Paco's cryptic words about the fire and Magart, and the way he ran when he saw that Floyd Fells was within earshot.

"I wonder if Paco might have really known something about Magart's death?"

Keller said, "I've tried to tell myself he didn't . . . but I don't really know. He sure acted like he had something to say—something he obviously wasn't willing to say in front of Fells. But why would he be scared of Fells in particular?"

"I don't know—but when you think about it, being scared of Fells might just be first cousin to being scared of David Weyburn."

Keller looked wryly at the sheriff. "Sounds like you're deliberately trying to pull Weyburn into this."

"Maybe I am. I don't make any bones about not trusting him, Jed, you know that. The man's trouble. It's written all over him." He paused. "Let me tell you something in confidence. I've already talked to the district attorney about Weyburn. I believe he thinks I'm crazy jealous of the man, but he owes me some favors and promised he'd check into Weyburn on the sly. He's got some good connections, and he's persistent. I've seen him learn more about a man than the man knows himself. I'll be eager to see if he finds anything on Weyburn."

Cooke walked to the stove, into which he tossed the dregs of his cup, rousing a steamy sizzle. "Weyburn's a real mystery to me. Living out there in that big house, away from everyone, everybody knowing him and liking him, but nobody really being close to him except for Fells. And did you know that every hand he has on his spread has been suspected at one time or another of being tied in with stock theft? Some even rode with the Wyeths in the past—can't prove it in every case, but I know it."

Keller finished his own coffee, mulling over the mystery. His thoughts went back to one of Cooke's past comments. "Till, who are the 'Old Boys' you talked about the other day?"

Cooke smiled coldly. "Let's put it this way: If Sheriff Weyburn turns out to be the sort I believe he is, you'll know soon enough who the Old Boys are. You might even be one of them. Now, Jed, if you'll excuse me, I've got to make a few rounds."

Keller pressed him for more explanation, but Cooke would say no more. Keller drove the wagon back to the ranch, wondering about the Old Boys and intending to ask Charlie Lilly about them. By the time he arrived, however, his thoughts had shifted to the work of the day, and Lilly was busy in the cookhouse, so the question remained unasked.

That night Keller did remember, and he called Lilly aside. Lilly's brows rose when he heard the query.

"The Old Boys? Indeed I can tell you something about the Old Boys. What I can't tell you is who they were, because nobody knows . . . or more exactly, nobody will tell."

"What do you know?"

"The Old Boys were a group of citizens, their identities well-hidden, who took matters into their own hands a couple of years ago when stock theft became a big problem. The situation, in fact, was much like it is now. The first thrust was no secret; several of the local ranchers and their hands joined with soldiers from Fort Cade and went looking for the Wyeths—the worst of the thieves—and took them on out in the hills about fifteen miles from the fort. Cutter Wyeth, unfortunately, didn't prove to be there, and the ones who were killed or taken prisoner were just small fish in the pond, so things didn't change much.

"Then, maybe a month later, the good people of Cade woke up to find a corpse hanging from the big mesquite tree at the north end of town. It was Curly Jones, a known member of Cutter Wyeth's group. There was a sign around his neck: 'Justice.' That's all it said. Then, over the next month, that tree played host to six more corpses, four of them stock thieves, the other two general lawbreakers who had been plaguing Cade. Till Cooke declared that he wouldn't put up with vigilance committees taking over the law . . . but I and plenty of others suspect he knew full well who made up that committee. In fact, some believe he led it himself. The 'Old Boys,' people began calling them. Word got out that no-accounts would not be tolerated by the Old Boys, and for about six months Cade was as trouble-free a place as you could hope to live. But it hasn't lasted. Where did you hear mention of the Old Boys, anyway?"

"From Till Cooke. He says the Old Boys might be back around soon . . . and that I might be among them."

"Do tell! And will you be?"

Keller shook his head. "Not me. I've never had use

for vigilance committees, and despite what you say, I doubt Till Cooke ever was part of one either."

"Perhaps not. He doesn't seem the type, I admit. But things about Cade are not always what they appear on the surface. A man who follows the written law by day might follow an unwritten one by night. Or maybe no law at all."

"Not me. I've killed on authority of the written law in my day. Sometimes on purpose. Once by accident . . . and I can't forget that one. I won't kill for any law again, written or unwritten."

"That's a humane ambition," Lilly said. "You obviously are a man of good conscience, Jed Keller."

Keller shook his head. "No. I'm just the opposite, and that's why I say what I do. I can't forget what it was to kill an innocent man, and I'll not risk killing another. I came to Cade to live a quiet life and live in peace, and I intend to do it. If the Old Boys come back 'round again, they'll not include Jed Keller in their number."

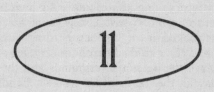

11

Three Months Later

Jed Keller was rolling a quirly when he heard the riders coming. He licked the paper into place, popped it onto his lip, and lit it as he strode toward the door. He paused long enough to remove his brand-new Winchester from the rack above the table—just in case the newcomers were not whom he anticipated.

He set the rifle aside as soon as he opened the door, for at the lead of the band was Till Cooke. Most of the fourteen men with him were cowhands from his ranch and a couple of others in the vicinity. Two, Larry Hite and Hal Allison, were ranch owners. And beside Cooke were two Tonkawas. All the men were well-armed and wore looks of grim determination.

"Hello, Jed."

"Till."

"I reckon you know who we're going after."

Keller nodded. "You have official approval?"

"Commander Wayne at Fort Cade has given his blessing. I think he'd rather see us do this than have to send out his own men."

"Has he got the authority to do that? Did you talk to the sheriff?"

Till Cooke spat contemptuously. "Believe it or not, I did, yesterday. So far he hasn't lifted a finger. Twenty-five horses stole altogether, and our fine new sheriff has let the thieves get a day's lead."

"So you're taking affairs into your own hands."

"There's no other way. You with us?"

Keller looked down, instincts battling with feelings. When he had come to the Brazos country, his desire had been to leave the pursuit of criminals and the enforcement of law in the hands of others—the hands of anyone except himself. Yet Cooke was right. The official sources of protection weren't working, and he, like almost every other rancher, was suffering for it. Since David Weyburn had taken office, theft of horses and stock had nearly doubled its already high rate—and Weyburn seemed determined to do nothing about it.

Keller looked up and nodded. "Give me ten minutes."

He strapped on a Colt and gathered ammunition and his sleeping gear while Charlie Lilly packed trail food. When he handed Keller the pouch, Keller said, "Charlie, there's enough here for two men."

"That's because I'm going too," Lilly said. He headed back to the bunkhouse on a lope, and within two minutes came out ready to ride.

They saddled horses and set off. The Tonkawas, long hair trailing behind them, rode in the lead. They were trackers beyond parallel, born of a people who lived by following the buffalo. Small in number, the Tonkawas had not been able to successfully vie with the Comanches for better range as the buffalo declined and moved, but this had only served to further sharpen their skills at tracking and survival. Keller was not surprised that the Tonkawas had joined this venture, for their tribe suffered from white thieves, just like the ranchers. Many a Tonkawa horse had been taken over the past two months.

They rode toward the west, for it was known that

the stock thieves—most certainly the Wyeths—had come this way. Cooke filled in Keller on the few details he possessed.

"We think they split up a few miles out," he said. "One of our Tonkawas yonder saw them and came to give the alert. There were may be eight of them altogether. One of the local sporting women is supposedly along with them, riding in a wagon. Her name's Nancy Scarlet, and she claims Cutter Wyeth as her man. Anyway, we think that part of the group took the stock northwest on a hard drive, and the rest, with the whore and the wagon, followed behind. I doubt they ever expected anybody would follow."

"Think we'll be able to catch them with the lead they've got?"

"We'll give it a devil of a try. I'm fed up, Jed. Good folk shouldn't be left high and dry to have their livelihood stole out from under them."

The Tonkawas found the trail easily, and this fueled the motivation of the pursuers greatly. Even Jed Keller, despite his initial trepidation, found lust for the chase rising in him. Cooke was right. Good people couldn't sit back and let themselves be rode over roughshod by thieves like the Wyeths.

They crossed the Brazos and continued, hardly resting. Night found them on the rolling plains many miles northwest of Cade. At last the weary horses and men stopped to make their camp.

Seated beside Cooke at one of the two campfires, Keller ate cold biscuits and beans and looked around at the group. "Is this the Old Boys, Till?"

Cooke shook his head. "Lord, no. But if things keep on like they are, Jed, you'll see the Old Boys."

Keller took another bite. Up until now he had firmly opposed any effort toward vigilante activity. Now he wasn't so convinced. Till Cooke's predictions of increased trouble with the advent of Weyburn in office had proven true. Might it take a stretching and bending of the law in order to set things right again? Even this posse, though bearing the informal approval of the Fort Cade commander, was legally questionable, a first move in the direction of vigilanteism.

Cooke's conversations tended to frequently drift around to the subject of Weyburn, and tonight was not an exception. "I have to admit, Weyburn has done a fair enough job in Cade itself," Cooke said. "It's safer on the streets than it has been in a long time. But beyond that—bah! I truly think the man's in league with Wyeth."

"But Weyburn's own spread has lost cattle. Horses too."

"What does that prove? If I was behind a ring of stock thieves, I'd make sure to hit myself enough times to make myself look innocent."

Keller hadn't thought of that. "So you think Weyburn has arranged thefts of his own stock?"

"It makes sense, don't it?"

"Yes. But is there any evidence of it?"

Cooke huffed and snorted. "There's my instincts."

"Instincts don't go far in a court of law."

"I ain't law anymore, Jed. Not that written law we've talked about, at least. I'm merely a rancher now, and a citizen, and I intend to see matters set right for the good folks about Cade, whatever it takes."

Cooke retired a few minutes later, and Keller rose to stretch his saddle-cramped legs and have a smoke. Charlie Lilly joined him.

"Did you hear what Cooke was saying?" Keller asked.

"Indeed I did. He's an angry man. ' "Revenge, revenge!" Timotheus cries; "See the Furies arise!" ' John Dryden."

Keller chuckled. Lilly had a poetic line for any occasion. Most of them so obscure they sailed right past, far above the heads of his less cultured listeners. Lilly took a lot of ribbing over his quotations, which seemed to distress him not at all.

"What do you think? You think Weyburn's as big a fraud as Till claims?"

Oddly, the question seemed to make Lilly uncomfortable. "I don't know much about Weyburn," Lilly said. "Before he began running for office, I never saw him except when he came to visit Mrs. Broadmore . . . the Broadmores, I should say." From Lilly's manner, Keller realized the man had said something unintended.

"Wait a minute, Charlie. Are you saying Weyburn came to call on Magart in particular?"

Lilly cleared his throat and fidgeted. "I don't wish to imply anything you might take as a slur against your sister, Jed."

"Charlie, say what you're thinking, straight out."

Lilly took Keller by the shoulder and moved him farther away from the group. Outside the range of the firelight, Keller could not see Lilly's expression well, but there was no mistaking the serious tone of his speech.

"Jed, David Weyburn was in love with Magart. And it wasn't a love that went unrequited."

"Hold on, here! You mean that Magart and Weyburn were—"

"Mrs. Broadmore lived a difficult life with a difficult husband. Folly Broadmore was crude and rough. Everyone on the ranch knew he beat her. Once he knocked her cold. He told the doctor she had fallen on the stairs."

"My God!"

"I've struggled for a long time over whether to say any of this to you," Lilly said. "After all, what good does it do you or Magart to dredge up a past that's sealed and unchangeable?"

"So why are you telling me now?"

"Because you have a right to know the truth. And

because I want to spare you any shock if ever you hear this from some other source."

Keller remembered his conversation with Weyburn in the Big Dakota, how Weyburn had spoken easily of his friendship with Magart, while only mentioning Folly Broadmore in passing. The notion that Weyburn might have had more than a friendly relationship with Magart Broadmore was novel and unsettling to Keller—yet it fit in with what little he knew. Magart had never been what folks might call a "proper" young lady, even in the days before she had met Folly Broadmore. Her rebelliousness had caused Mark Keller to clamp down hard on his wayward daughter, which only made Magart all the more defiant. Keller had always thought she married as much to assert her independence from their father as out of any real love for Folly Broadmore, who had been a most unlovable character.

Might Magart have been an unfaithful wife to Broadmore? Knowing her ways and character, Keller couldn't honestly declare it impossible.

Later, as he lay on his bedroll, Keller found the threads of his thoughts coming together in a distressing way. There was Paco the Mex and his cryptic hints that he knew something secret about the Broadmore ranch fire, something he was afraid for Fells to hear him reveal. And then, right after that, Paco had vanished, and had remained absent since. Add to that Weyburn's own mention of "friendship" with Magart, and Lilly's suspicions that the two had carried on a secret romantic affair . . .

Keller went to sleep with a new conviction in mind: Somehow the fire at the Broadmore ranch and the deaths of Magart and her husband had something to do with Weyburn. There was a connection—a connection not yet clear. And in some way, Paco the Mex had known what that connection was. Keller recalled how Weyburn himself had quizzed him so directly about the reason for his initial tangle with Paco, as if eager to

learn what Paco had said. And now Paco was gone altogether. Perhaps he had absconded out of fear of Fells or
Weyburn. Or perhaps he was dead.

Despite his exhaustion from the day's hard ride, Jed
Keller didn't sleep well that night.

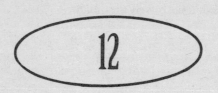

12

The morning came in cloudy, the sky gray and hanging low like a cavern ceiling. The wind drove violently across the grasslands, making the mesquite trees tremble and generating in Jed Keller the feeling that something of import was about to happen.

The two Tonkawas, riding ahead of the others, were the first to see the wagon. Crippled by a broken wheel, it sat unhitched in the midst of the rolling land, and on its seat, managing to stay aboard despite the slant caused by the wagon's sitting on one wheel and one hub, was a woman in a bright yellow dress cut low in the bustline. She held an open laced parasol above her head as though the day were sunny. The men could hear her cussing in a stream that knew no end, and the man whose name she was damning was none other than Cutter Wyeth.

"Well, look there," Till Cooke said. "Nancy Scarlet herself. It looks like old Cutter Wyeth has run off on her."

Till clicked his tongue and advanced up to the wagon. Nancy Scarlet, her face blotched and her eyes red from crying, quit cussing as Cooke approached. "Hello, Sheriff," she said.

"I ain't sheriff no more," Cooke replied. "Did they leave you stranded out here, Nancy?"

She launched into another tirade that featured several obscenities that sounded particularly vile spoken by a feminine voice. Once again Cutter Wyeth was on the receiving end of the onslaught—not that he was anywhere close by to hear it.

"Was Cutter driving this wagon?" Cooke asked.

"It was him, and him that left me sitting here on my butt!" she declared. The wind suddenly caught her parasol and threatened to turn it inside out. Trying to close it, she lost her perch on the slanting wagon seat and slid down sideways and completely out of the wagon. Nevertheless she landed on her feet.

"She's agile," one of the cowboys in the group said.

"Don't I know it!" another muttered in a wistful way that drew glances from the other men. He turned red and ducked his face.

"So that's where you been going them Friday nights," one of the others said.

"Sheriff," said Nancy, clinging to Cooke's former title, "I want you to go arrest Cutter. He was going to take me off and marry me, but when the wagon broke its wheel he just left me. He said he'd be back to fix it, and I needed to guard it for him! Can you believe that? He wants me to guard his wagon! He just wanted to be rid of me, that's all."

"Did he know he was being followed?"

"Hell, no! That was just his talk, his excuse for dumping me off! He'd been saying all along that there wouldn't be nobody following."

"Did he say anything to indicate that he has some sort of deal with David Weyburn? Something to indicate Weyburn is in league with him, you know, cooperating with him in stealing stock?"

Nancy's blank look indicated that the notion was new to her. Cooke looked disappointed; obviously he had hoped the prostitute could verify his suspicions—

suspicions that were increasingly voiced by many others, particularly cattlemen.

Keller rode forward a few paces. "Where is Wyeth now?"

"At the old cabin in Salty Basin," she said. There was no hesitation; she was a woman who felt betrayed and who would therefore betray in turn. "They keep the horses there, until they sell them to somebody up in Kansas."

"Salty Basin," Cooke said. "A thieve's hole from way on back. Hal, why don't you escort Miss Scarlet back to Cade. As for the rest of us, by grabs, let's go pay Cutter Wyeth a visit!"

The horses were still there, corraled behind the little two-room cabin. The doors and shutters of the house were open, for the day was warm even though overcast, the heat slowly thinning out the clouds. Outside, a big fire blazed beneath a black kettle and coffeepot. Nearby, a creek ran in a course cut deep into the soil.

Cooke checked his rifle one last time and glanced at the men stationed all around him, hiding behind the trees, brush, and rocks along the slope leading down to the house. Keller gauged the range and found it a little long for his liking, but to go closer would mean leaving cover behind.

"Just how are we going to do this?" Charlie Lilly asked. He was stationed on one side of Cooke; Keller was on the other.

"I wouldn't think we'd want them to fight, unless it comes to it," Keller said. "What we do, first and foremost, is get our horses back."

"I've got a little more than that in mind," Cooke mumbled.

Keller didn't understand him. "What'd you say, Till?"

"Nothing. Nothing."

"I got an idea of what to do," Keller said.

He outlined a plan, and found it matched what Cooke already had in mind. Having been trained by Cooke, Keller naturally thought along similar strategic lines.

"I'll go," Cooke said. "I can slip around and—"

"You'll stay here," Keller said. "I'll go."

"I'm in charge here," Cooke said.

"Yeah, but I'm younger—and faster." And with that Keller was up, moving at a quick lope with his head low, circling around the slope toward the corral, staying just out of sight.

By the time he reached the corral—completing his circuitous route had taken six minutes—Keller was winded but confident his plan would work. The single window on the side of the house facing the corral was closed, and the only obvious evidence of human presence at the place was smoke rising from the fire on the other side, and the muffled sound of men's voices inside.

Keller dropped to the ground when he heard a door open. There was no cover here except the grass at the edge of the corral and the conglomerate legs of the horses as they milled in the corral between Keller and the house.

Keller hoped that whoever had left the house was simply going to the cook fire to check the progress of the meal. He was disheartened to see two men stride around the side of the house, however, and head for the corral.

"I'll show the one I'm talking about, Cutter," one of the men was saying. "She's a beaut—finest I've seen, prettier even than that dun filly last fall. You remember that one?"

"Yep."

Keller's fingers wrapped around the stock of his rifle. He couldn't see enough of the men to know if they were armed; he would have to assume they were. Obviously one of them was Cutter Wyeth himself, and he would not likely give up easily. He had stolen so many horses and rustled so many cattle in his time that he would almost surely face the noose if caught.

This was not part of the plan; Keller had not anticipated anyone coming out of the house, at least, not until he had opened the corral gate and stampeded the horses. At that point those in the house would certainly rush out—and Till Cooke and the others could sweep down, overwhelm them, and take them in. If all went well, not a shot would have to be fired.

Wyeth and the man with him drew closer, closer . . . and Keller was almost to the desperate point of leaping up and demanding their surrender when they stopped, apparently having located the horse they sought. As they conversed about the form and strength of the animal—which bore the brand of Larry Hite's spread—Keller lowered his head and took a deep but silent breath. The plan might work after all. Wyeth and his companion would talk, then return to the house, and then he could proceed to free the horses as planned.

But fortune had other things in mind. Just as the two stock thieves were about to turn back toward the cabin, the sun broke through the clouds for the first time that day, pouring golden light across the entire little creek basin in which the cabin stood. And to Keller's misfortune, one of the rays glinted on the shiny hammer of his new rifle.

It was the tiniest glint of light, but it caught Wyeth's eye and aroused his suspicion. Conversation stopped, the horses began moving aside, and Keller saw Wyeth's booted feet stepping in his direction among the conglomeration of hooves.

"Wyeth!"

The yell came from up the slope, and it was Till Cooke's voice. Wyeth spun, and that, combined with the shifting of the horses, allowed Keller a clear view of him through the clumps of grass below the corral fence. Wyeth was indeed armed, but only with a pistol—

hardly a weapon to make much difference against the armed cattlemen above.

"Who's there?" Wyeth yelled.

"It's Till Cooke, Wyeth! Drop that pistol!"

Wyeth refused with an oath, and Keller chose that moment to rise. He slammed the rifle stock against his shoulder, lined up the sight on Wyeth's midsection, and advised Wyeth that obedience to Cooke's command might be prudent.

Wyeth had obviously been taken by complete surprise—as had his partner, who carried no weapon and had stuck his hands into the air at Cooke's first yell.

Wyeth swore and dropped the pistol. Keller moved in, planning to take Wyeth hostage and use him as a human shield as he edged him up the slope and away from the house. Unfortunately, some of the cattlemen on the rise were young and overeager; three of them leaped from their fighting positions and came bounding down toward Keller and the two outlaws.

"No!" Keller yelled. The echo of the word was drowned out in the roar of rifle fire from the cabin. The closest cowboy jerked and fell, blood running out of his side. A moment later the man with him also fell, crying out and grabbing his leg, his rifle rattling to the earth. The wounded men began scrambling back up the slope to safety. Wyeth, meanwhile, did a flat fall onto the ground, regained his pistol and fired sideways at Jed, all in a fluid continuum of motion. It was a graceful and effective exercise, but his aim was not good and the slug did no more than rip the hat off Keller's head.

Gunfire peppered in both directions as the cattlemen and the cabin's occupants faced off. The unarmed bandit who had come out with Wyeth ran for the safety of the creek bank, a move that seemed quite sensible to Keller as well. He loped off toward the creek as Wyeth sent another slug winging vainly after him, then turned his attention to the slope above.

Keller made it to the creek and leaped over the edge

of the cut bank, splashing into the water. He heard a curse and looked over his shoulder to see the unarmed outlaw, who had been in the process of moving belly down into the water, below bank level.

"Hold it there—stay on your belly, hands behind your head, and face down," Keller barked.

"I'll drown!" the man declared.

"Then turn your head to the side, fool! But one move after that, and you're dead."

The battle, meanwhile, was growing fiercer. Wyeth was not at the corral anymore, apparently having made it back to the house or perhaps to some other place of cover. Meanwhile, some of the cattlemen were coming down the slope, edging toward the cabin as they made use of what meager cover they could find.

"God, they'll shoot us all, and if they don't shoot us, they'll hang us!" the unarmed outlaw wailed. His mouth was half submerged in the creek water, which gave his words a blubbering quality.

Keller glanced disgustedly at his prisoner and felt torn between the need to move back into the battle and the need to guard this man, who now was beginning to sniffle pitifully.

Keller made his choice. He levered his rifle, turned to the man and said, "Get up and start running."

"You're going to shoot me, ain't you! You're going to shoot me in the back while I run!"

"Maybe I will. Or would you rather I shoot you in the head, where you lie? Get up and run!"

The man did as he was told, darting like a rabbit across the rolling prairie and up the far edge of the basin, until Keller saw him no more. No doubt the man had expected every step to be his last.

Keller took a deep breath, rose, and darted into the battle. He saw Wyeth, crouched behind a scrubby tree near the corral, still fighting with his pistol. The outlaw was so distracted that Keller realized he could probably reach him from behind before he ever realized anyone was coming.

He decided to do just that. Shifting left to put himself squarely behind Wyeth, he began loping forward with wide, careful strides. Meanwhile, Wyeth was taking aim around the trunk of the tree . . . and then he fired, just as Keller saw who his target was.

Till Cooke. Through the smoke of Wyeth's pistol Keller saw his old mentor crumple to the ground. A shiver of horror overwhelmed Keller, and he surged forward with a yell.

Wyeth, still crouched, twisted around just in time to see the butt of Keller's rifle come straight into his forehead, driving the back of his skull against the tree with the force of a sledge.

Keller didn't pause to examine the results of his work. He darted past to Cooke, ignoring the continuing gunfire on all sides.

"Till!" he yelled. "Till, are you alive?"

13

Cooke was pushing himself to his feet even as Keller reached him. "I'm fine, fine. He didn't even hit me; I just stumbled—look out!"

Keller, not knowing what Cooke had just seen or how to react to so imprecise a warning, instinctively ducked, putting his hands on his head. It was the correct move, for it saved him from losing his brains to a rifle wildly swung by one of the outlaws who had run out of bullets and now was panicked. Till Cooke drew his pistol and shot the outlaw in the knee, driving him down howling. Keller turned and wrenched the empty rifle from the fallen man as he lost consciousness.

Keller and Cooke, both on their feet again, headed for some nearby rocks, diving behind them as slugs spanged around them. They came up firing, Keller marveling to himself the entire while. *Why am I here? I came to Texas to escape this kind of thing—and now I'm fighting for my life.*

The battle quickly wound down, and the cattlemen emerged victorious. When Cooke and Keller converged with the others around the little cabin, they discovered their force had suffered no deaths. For that matter, neither had the surprised stock thieves. Unfortunately, the confusion had given one break to the besieged outlaws. Five of them together had made a coordinated run for some of the stolen horses and ridden away pell-mell, slugs whizzing over them. A fifth escapee was the man Keller had let run away down at the creek, and a sixth, the man Cooke had shot in the knee, who had managed to drag himself around to the far side of the house and now was nowhere to be found. The presumption was that he too had mounted a horse and gotten away.

The cattlemen were astounded and disgusted that so many had gotten away. Still, the results hadn't been a failure, for most of the stolen stock had been recovered —and best of all, one of the two remaining prisoners was Cutter Wyeth himself.

Wyeth had regained consciousness only to find himself tied up and surrounded by the grim-faced cattlemen. The man's ugly face paled beneath his scraggly whiskers, and his drooping eye narrowed to a dark slit.

Till Cooke, who as sheriff had spent long, frustrated years unable to snare the region's worst stock rustler, advanced on Cutter Wyeth and looked with dark satisfaction in his face. The scene around the cabin fell quiet and pregnant with anticipation; the cattlemen moved in close to hear what Till Cooke had to say.

He had just opened his mouth to speak when Wyeth spat on him. Cooke took the foulness in the face without even a flinch. Slowly, never letting his gaze drop from Wyeth's, he dug a cloth from his pocket and wiped off the spittle.

Wyeth grinned in a typically twisted fashion, his mouth curling like a drying leaf. "Well, Cooke, you finally trapped your rat," he said. "It's been a hell of a run I've given you, huh?"

"That you have. But every rat gets caught sooner or later."

"So what will you do with me?"

"Hang you, I reckon. Here and now."

Keller stepped forward. "What?"

"I said we were going to hang him."

"No," Keller said firmly. "We're not."

Cooke pivoted his head and looked at Keller in disbelief. "What do you mean, no? This is Cutter Wyeth himself! You saying he don't deserve the noose?"

"Of course he does. But it's not our place to do that job. You said yourself that this group isn't the Old Boys. I won't take part in lynching a man."

Cooke swore and threw his hands skyward. "So what do you think we ought to do? Take him to Weyburn and watch him walk free?"

"I don't think Weyburn could just let him go. Too many eyes on him for that. He'd be obliged to see him through to justice."

Cooke replied, "I never thought you to be so simple, Jed. These here men ain't exactly peace-loving Pennsylvania Shakers! Weyburn ain't to be trusted—especially not with a man he's almost dead certain working with in the background."

Wyeth pulled at his ropes and twitched the right side of his face. "I don't know no Weyburn," he said.

"Shut up," Cooke barked at the outlaw, still looking angrily at Keller. "Jed, there's nobody out here but cattlemen, every one of us victims of this here maggot." He waved contemptuously at Wyeth. "I say let's squash him, then keep our mouths shut."

"What about the other prisoner? You going to hang him too?"

"I don't see why not."

The other prisoner, a tall man made of beard and gristle, jerked at the ropes that bound him. "I ain't part of no stock thieving!" he bellowed. "I'm a buffalo hunter, and that's all! I come here to play cards with my cousin, and that's the God's truth!"

One of the cowboys said, "I think he's telling it true. I seen him before in Cade, down at the hide yard. And unless I counted wrong, I saw nine men down here at one time or another, and there was only eight thieves. So one had to be an extra."

This development seemed to knock Cooke off balance, so Keller pressed the issue. "See, Till? You can't hang a man you don't know is guilty. You'll have to take him back alive, no matter what you do to Wyeth, and when you do, you'll have a witness to your lynching."

"I say hang them both," Cooke growled. "He was with them, so he's guilty in my book."

"That's not the Till Cooke I worked with, saying that," Keller said. "The Till Cooke I worked with was always a man of law."

"You may not know Till Cooke so bloody well as you think!" Cooke shot back. "But I know you, Jed, and I know what's behind this high moral tone you're setting! You're still bowel-bound over that fellow you killed years ago! That's it, ain't it? That old memory has eat away at your nerve until it's gone!"

Keller clamped his teeth together, anger rising. "It's got nothing to do with anything except following the law," he retorted. "You used to believe in that yourself —in case you've forgotten."

"If our great-grandfathers had thought like you think, we'd all still be sipping English tea," Cooke said. "There's a law higher than that on the books, and sometimes it's got to be followed."

Keller forced himself to calm down. "Till, all I'm asking is that we not become murderers in the name of justice." He pointed at the self-professed buffalo hunter. It took great effort to speak calmly, but he did it. "If this man is innocent, it'd be his blood on our hands forever if we lynch him. And while I'm talking, let me be full square with you. Yes, I do think back on that poor fellow I killed—and because of what happened that day, I know what it is to kill a man wrongly. I won't be part of doing that again."

Cooke remained silent, apparently thinking. One of

the other cattlemen cleared his throat and uncomfortably contributed: "I don't much like the idea of hanging anybody without a trial." A couple of others murmured agreement.

At length Cooke sighed and nodded. He turned to Wyeth. "Looks like you've escaped the rope—for now," he said. Then, to Keller: "Jed, if we take Wyeth in to Weyburn, I guarantee you Weyburn won't do a thing but find an excuse to let him go."

"Then let's not take them to Weyburn."

"Where, then?"

"To Fort Cade. Turn them over to the commander."

The cattlemen looked among themselves. "Sounds good to me," one commented, and others followed suit, seeming relieved.

"Till?"

The former sheriff nodded. "I reckon I can go along with that. Though I ain't forgetting that you crossed me on this, Jed. I ain't forgetting."

Keller was too relieved to worry about Cooke's last statement. He glanced at Wyeth, who was still very white from realizing how closely he had brushed the hangman's noose. Keller's nose twitched, he glanced down and grinned.

"Gentlemen," he said. "Take a look—it appears the daring Mr. Cutter Wyeth has peed his pants."

Indeed, a warm, dark ring had spread down the front of the outlaw's trousers; he himself hadn't even noticed it, wrapped up as he was in the preceding debate over his fate. Now his blanched face went red and he fumed as his captors laughed at and mocked him.

"Cooke!" Wyeth said.

Till Cooke wheeled, stalked up to Wyeth and faced him at a distance no more than ten inches. "What, maggot?"

"I'll remember it was you who would have hanged

me, Cooke. Keep your eyes open . . . one of these days there'll come a settling up. You can count on it."

Cooke said nothing. Then, abruptly, he spat in Wyeth's face just as Wyeth had spat in his.

"You'll hang yet, Wyeth," he said. "And when you do, I'll be there to see you twitch your last. And believe me, I'll appreciate the show."

He stomped away, leaving Wyeth tied up and trying vainly to wipe off his face with a hunched shoulder.

"Come on, gents," Keller said to those around him. "Let's patch up the hurt ones and head to Fort Cade."

The men moved immediately in response. None of them, Keller included, thought about it, but something important had just occurred: Jed Keller had just taken on a new status. He had vied with Till Cooke's unofficial authority and won; he had given a directive and they had responded.

Without trying to, Jed Keller had just gained the status of leadership.

14

David Weyburn shifted in his saddle and felt tension ripple through the tight muscles of his back. Putting his hands on the saddle horn, he leaned forward and wished he could find a comfortable position.

His eyes darted from side to side, noting the men with him. Unlike Till Cooke, who had operated the sheriff's office with a force of only three deputies, Weyburn had hired a force of eight, an expense he had justified to the county's governing body on the grounds that a larger force would allow him to make a greater impact on stock theft at the outlying ranches. He could send deputies on constant patrol rounds throughout the county, giving the outlying ranches greater access to the law.

In fact, Weyburn had sent men out on such rounds only twice since coming into office. He liked keeping his deputies—all of them men who had worked for him in far less legal capacities in the past—close at hand. It countered the rising sense of discomfort in office that had plagued him since he had been sworn in.

It was most disconcerting; Weyburn had expected to ease into the post as comfortably as a foot sliding into a familiar old boot. David Weyburn and the post of county sheriff had seemed a made-to-order match. As sheriff he could exercise official authority and power, keep control of forces that otherwise might be used against him, and thus work in league with Wyeth and his ring of stock thieves—all without fear of detection. As the proverbial wolf guarding the henhouse, he could feel secure and powerful. Instead he felt increasingly ill at ease.

Mostly it had to do with the district attorney, who reportedly had been asking some disconcerting questions about the new sheriff ever since he came into office. That was Till Cooke's doing, Weyburn figured; he knew how Cooke distrusted him, and guessed that he must have cashed in some due favor by getting the district attorney to check him out. Weyburn hated Cooke for it. Hated him, but didn't know how to deal with him.

Today he would have to deal with Till Cooke, if what Floyd Fells had told him was true. Fells had come riding hard to Weyburn's office, telling him that Cooke and a group of cattlemen and cowboys had gone off on their own after Cutter Wyeth and a herd of stolen horses. Now Cooke's group had been spotted returning, with Wyeth in custody.

This created quite a predicament for Weyburn. As sheriff, it would be his duty to imprison Wyeth, but as Wyeth's secret partner, he couldn't actually bring the law to bear on the man. Even now, as he, his deputies, and several of his ranch hands waited for the cattlemen and their prisoners to come into view, Weyburn wasn't sure how he was going to handle this matter.

Weyburn lifted his chin and spied out across the rolling plains. A lone rider, one of his own men, was approaching. He rode up to Weyburn. "They're heading toward Fort Cade!" he said breathlessly. "They're trying to pass us by! If we're going to intercept them, we'll have to move fast!"

Fort Cade? Weyburn hadn't expected that. Were

Till Cooke's suspicions about him so strong that he wouldn't bring his prisoners into county custody? It made chilling sense, and Weyburn cursed himself for not anticipating such a move.

He couldn't allow the military authorities to take in Wyeth. If Wyeth wound up in their hands, he would be out of his own reach; Weyburn knew he would be unable either to aid Wyeth or control him. Left to vie for himself, Wyeth might start spilling the facts about their secret alliance. . . .

No. He wouldn't let that happen. Weyburn lifted his hand. "Ride!" he ordered. And they set off, angling across the plains in a cloud of dust.

"Look yonder!" Jed Keller said, pointing. But Till Cooke needed no tip-off; he had already seen the oncoming horsemen.

"That's Weyburn in the lead," he said. "Weyburn and his bunch of deputized scoundrels, come to claim their prisoner, I'll betcha. I wonder how he knew?"

"You can't hide much in this country," Keller replied. "They've probably been spying out for us. You going to turn Wyeth over to him?"

Cooke's tone betrayed how distasteful conversation with Keller was for him at the moment. "Not by any stretch. I'll see Cutter Wyeth through that fort gate and into military custody before I let go of him."

"Think we could make a run and reach the fort before Weyburn gets here?"

"Not a chance. He's coming too fast. And what does it matter? This might be just what's needed to prove once and for all that Weyburn's what I think he is."

And so they waited. Weyburn's band grew closer. It slowed only when it became apparent that Cooke, Keller, and company were not going to attempt any scramble for Fort Cade. By the time Weyburn was within talking distance, he rode at a slow lope. He eyed the group as he approached—his gaze lingering an extra second or two on Keller—then came to a halt before Cooke. Weyburn, Keller noticed, had not looked at Wyeth at all.

For several seconds silence reigned. Keller found it fascinating and surprising to see that Weyburn, despite the badge on his vest and his band of surly armed deputies, seemed the underdog in this situation. He was amused when he detected Weyburn swallowing again and again—dry-mouthed, Keller figured, from nervousness.

"What's the nature of this band?" Weyburn asked. His voice sounded a little higher and more strained than normal.

"We're just a group of private citizens, operating under the authority of Fort Cade . . . Sheriff." Cooke put sarcastic emphasis on Weyburn's title.

"That man there appears to be Cutter Wyeth."

"You ought to know." The comment evoked a murmur of laughter from the cynical cattlemen. Weyburn's expression grew darker.

"Where are you taking these men?" Weyburn asked.

"Fort Cade. We intend to turn him over to authorities who are trustworthy and honest, and who empowered us to act."

"Fort Cade has no authority to mandate any venture like this. I'm the sheriff of this county. This is a matter under my jurisdiction."

"I don't think so. It's my opinion that you're of similar ilk to the outlaw himself, and likely in league with him. To turn him over to you would be idiocy. If you've got a squabble with the fort commander, take it up with the Army."

Weyburn was beginning to get mad now, and the effect was actually helpful to him, for it enabled him to overcome his case of nerves. "Listen to me, Mr. Cooke: I'll not have you and your—your . . . gang making like a bunch of vigilantes. You think you're the Old Boys? Well, I'll have none of that in my county. Those days are past."

"The Old Boys? That's not us, Sheriff. The Old Boys are long gone . . . though I confess that may be regrettable, given what we're forced to deal with these days. Not that I advocate vigilanteism, Sheriff Weyburn. No sir, not me."

Weyburn said, "That's a more open question than you might have us believe, Cooke. I've heard a widespread opinion that the sheriff who used to send out such loud warnings to the Old Boys to cease and desist their kind of 'justice' was in fact himself the leader of that very group."

"You can't believe all you hear. A good lawman ought to know that. But I suppose 'good lawman' doesn't necessarily apply to you, does it?"

Keller couldn't squelch his smile; Cooke was managing to insult Weyburn with almost every sentence. Weyburn wasn't missing it either, and it made him more angry. He reined in a little closer to Cooke.

"Listen to me, old man: I know you don't respect me. I know you're jealous of me because I hold your old job—jealous even though it was you who stepped down. You think you're going to ride roughshod over me, mock me before my own men, and act like a law unto yourself. Well, you can damn well forget it, Cooke. I know what you've done here. You've bypassed the elected authorities and gone out on what amounts to a vigilante raid. Perhaps you've even killed some men that I don't yet know about. Obviously, you've taken a couple of prisoners. Well, they're my prisoners now, and you can hand them over . . . or face charges as a vigilante."

That threat generated some somber glances among the cattlemen. Driven by anger and the desire to avenge themselves on the stock thieves, they were realizing only now that their actions might have legal ramifications.

Cooke's expression was a sight to see. "You dare to threaten me, rascal? You're part and parcel with scum like Wyeth."

"I'm sheriff, that's what I am. I have the force of law behind me, and you no longer do. Now, turn over the prisoners."

The self-professed buffalo hunter, his hands lashed to his saddle horn, said, "I ain't done a thing, Sheriff. They took me prisoner and almost hung me—and I swear I ain't done a thing!"

Weyburn seized the opportunity to tighten the squeeze on Cooke. To the buffalo hunter he said, "Are you willing to state that under oath, if called upon?"

"Yes sir, I am."

One of Weyburn's deputies said, "He's telling the truth. That's J. N. Tucker. He is a buffalo man, just like he says. He's no thief."

"I don't know one end of a cow from another," Tucker said.

Keller turned to Cooke. "Till, we're going to have to do what he says."

Cooke's glare upon Keller was hot enough to burn. "Do what he says? Not me! I'm taking Wyeth to Fort Cade. Hell, it was your idea, Jed! You going to back out on me now? You going to defy me again?"

"There's no choice, Till. Weyburn's the sheriff, like it or not. If he wants to make trouble for us, he can do it." Keller faced Weyburn. "Besides, this will give Weyburn a chance to prove he's the honest lawman he claims to be. If he's square, he'll see that Wyeth gets what's coming to him. If he doesn't, we'll know he's the fraud we think him to be."

Weyburn examined Keller with that same unusual interest he always gave the man. "Tell me, Mr. Keller— what has poisoned you against me?"

Through Keller's mind ran the list of events that had aroused his suspicions: the encounters with Paco the Mex, Weyburn's own insistent questioning about

Paco and the Broadmore fire, Paco's disappearance, and his knowledge that Weyburn and Magart had likely been carrying on a love affair. None of these were things that needed saying in the present context, so Keller replied, "The time may come when you and me will have to have a good talk."

Cooke spoke. "All right, Weyburn. You win. Take our prisoners. We'll be watching to see how you deal with them. If there's anything wrong in how they're handled, there'll be no lack of response. Of that I assure you."

"What's your plan, Cooke? To bring back the Old Boys? To ride in the dark and dispense your private notion of justice with a rope, but without benefit of judge and jury?"

"It's you who keeps trying to tie me to the Old Boys, Weyburn. Keep up that kind of slander, and I just may challenge you to prove your words in a court of law."

Weyburn had no more to say. He collected the buffalo hunter and Wyeth—who bore a look of relief he couldn't disguise despite all his efforts—and turned with his men toward Cade. Keller watched them ride away.

"I'm willing to bet that Cutter Wyeth will be gone from Weyburn's cell before sundown tomorrow," Keller said.

"Then why did you force my hand, Jed? What's got into you? What's turned you so against me?" Cooke's tone indicated a level of anger that startled Keller.

"Till, if we hadn't gone along, he would have put charges on us—charges that would have stuck."

"You're soft, Jed. Soft and scared as a woman. I never would have thought it of you. I thought I knew you. Reckon I was wrong. You've changed."

"It's you who's changed, Till. You used to be a man who believed in the law."

At that, Cooke swore, turned away, clicked his tongue, and rode off toward his ranch, his every movement indicating clearly that he neither wanted nor expected any company along the way.

Keller watched him go, and felt sad and angry at the same time. The sorrow came from having his old mentor take such a low view of him; the anger came from knowing that Cooke would go home and do his best to fill Claire with ill will toward him as well. He could stand having Till Cooke think ill of him. Having Claire O'Keefe do the same was quite a different thing.

Keller rode home in declining spirits. Charlie Lilly's horse plodded along beside him. "Well, it was a noble venture, even if Wyeth did wind up in Weyburn's hands. The efforts of good men bear their own rewards, thankfully. To quote Thomas Gray: 'Some bold adventurers disdain the limits of their little reign, and unknown regions dare descry—' "

"Charlie," Keller interrupted. "Here's a poem for you, very short and to the point, and I hope you take it to heart: Shut up, dear Charles, shut up."

He spurred his gelding and rode on ahead, leaving a taken-aback Lilly gaping after him.

15

Keller crossed the rise and saw Claire out by the chicken pen. It was remarkable that even so mundane an activity as feeding hens became fascinating to watch when performed by such a woman. He felt a familiar warmth rise inside him, only to have it cooled by the fear that Till Cooke's anger might have spread to his niece.

She straightened and put her hand to her brow, shielding her eyes as she saw him. Keller waved, and she waved back. *So far, so good,* he thought. *At least she isn't ignoring me or running into the house for a shotgun.*

"Hello, Jed."

"Evening, Claire. How you been?"

"Very well, though things have been . . . difficult, I guess you could say, around here the last day or two." Keller was between Claire and the setting sun, so she kept her hand at her brow and squinted in a way that he found most alluring. As a matter of fact, he couldn't think of a thing about Claire that wasn't alluring.

"Till's still mad at me?"

Claire glanced back at the house, then came a step or two closer to Keller. "He's more than mad. You defied him. To him, that's betrayal."

"How do you feel about it?"

"I'm glad you did what you did. It's always best to operate within the law, and Uncle Till himself knows that, when his temper doesn't get in the way of his sense. But we shouldn't be talking like this; if he sees us, he'll probably figure I'm betraying him too." Keller detected an edge of exasperation in the words. Apparently, life in the household of Till Cooke had taken a certain toll on Claire's patience since last he saw her.

Cooke emerged from the house, filling the door in a way that few men could. "Well, look who's here!" he said in a noticeably sarcastic tone. "Mr. Take-Charge, Turn-'em-Over-to-Weyburn Keller!"

Keller dismounted and dropped the reins. The horse, already cropping the grass, was trusty and would not wander far. "Till, I came to see if I was still welcome on your land. I think I've already got my answer."

"What? Now you're trying to make me feel bad?" Cooke said. "I never said nothing about you not being welcome. Come in." The words sounded like banter, but without the covert affection that goes with such.

Claire took Keller's arm as they advanced to the house, and Keller appreciated the support subtly indicated in the gesture as much as the affection it also spoke of.

Cooke was obviously still angry, but something intangible had changed. Over coffee the two men talked, and Keller could tell that Cooke's thoughts had traveled past the disagreement over Wyeth that had divided them. There was an underlying restlessness in Cooke's manner, and an aura of distraction about him. Cooke fidgeted like a man waiting to meet an old lover, or an heir awaiting the reading of a will that could make him rich.

Keller had not come intending to stay long, so after a few minutes of conversation, he rose to leave. He had assumed that Cooke's willingness to talk would make him feel better about things. He didn't feel better. Till

Cooke had talked with him, but not to him. The senior man's words might as well have been aimed at the corner for all the feeling that came through them.

"Take a walk with me before you go," Claire invited Keller. "This is a beautiful time of the evening for a stroll, don't you think?"

Outside, she clung to his arm and began talking about Cooke as soon as they were out of earshot of the house.

"He's been coming and going ever since he got back from chasing Wyeth and his rustlers," Claire said. "And this afternoon Ben Potts came over from the Lucky Y, and they talked for nearly an hour—shutting up real fast whenever they thought I might hear. What does it mean?"

Keller said, "I don't know for sure, but I'm willing to make a likely guess. I believe Till is reorganizing the Old Boys."

"The Old Boys?"

"Yes. Vigilantes that cleaned up the area a few years back. Nobody knew who they were, other than they reportedly included some of the finer male citizens. And I'm on pretty solid ground when I tell you that your uncle was the leader. Sheriff by day, vigilante leader by night."

"Do you really think so? I hate to consider such a thing!"

"So do I, Claire. But the fact is, Till has strongly hinted to me since I first arrived that the Old Boys were going to return to action, with me included. Or that's what he wanted."

"But he hasn't asked you?"

"Of course not, not while he's mad at me. I guess he doesn't think anymore that I have the right sort of spirit. It's not only because of our argument over Wyeth and Weyburn either. It goes back to something that happened years ago, in Missouri, when I first went to work as Till's deputy. I killed an innocent man, and it almost ended my career. In the end, that killing did end it, because it haunted me until I finally laid down my badge." Succinctly and quietly, he told her the story of the shooting in the bank. "When Till started talking about the Old Boys, I told him I didn't want to be part of it. It touched too much on that bad memory."

"But you went with him after the Wyeths. . . ."

"I know. But that wasn't intended to be a lynch mob, though it was clear at the end that Till was ready to turn it into one."

"Poor Uncle Till . . . he becomes obsessed when he gets a particular notion. It seems now that all he can think about is stock theft and David Weyburn. He despises the man so."

"I know. He believes Weyburn is in league with the Wyeths, which he very well may be. And the truth is, I'm as wary of Weyburn as Till is, and not just about stock theft." He cleared his throat. "Claire, may I tell you something in confidence?"

"Of course."

"I think David Weyburn was somehow involved with my sister's death."

"Involved? You think he killed her?"

"I didn't say that—the truth is, I don't know what I mean. It's just that since I first came to Cade, things have happened, things have been said. . . . Weyburn himself has acted peculiar around me, unless I'm just letting my imagination get out of hand. But just this week, Charlie Lilly told me something about Magart and Weyburn. They were having a love affair right before the fire that killed her and Folly Broadmore."

"A love affair!"

"That's right." He told her the story, starting with his own drunken attack on Paco the Mex and including everything thereafter. "So you see, I've got nothing that really holds together, not even enough to set up a clear suspicion. I don't even know what it is I suspect Weyburn of! But there's something there. I know there is."

"So Weyburn may be just as shady as Uncle Till thinks."

"I suspect he is. One thing you've got to say for Till, he has good instincts. He can judge a man by looking at him, and get it right nine times out of ten."

"If you feel that way, why did you let Wyeth be turned over to Weyburn?"

"There was a second man in our custody and no clear indication he was guilty of anything. Weyburn could have used that to cause us trouble if we had defied him and gone on to Fort Cade. And anyway, putting Wyeth in his hands is a sort of test. If Weyburn is honest, like he claims, he'll treat Wyeth like the criminal he is. If he lets Wyeth weasel out, then no cattleman in this county will trust him. It really puts Weyburn in a hot spot, having Wyeth in his cell."

"Is Wyeth still locked up?"

"As of this afternoon, yes. It'll be interesting to see if it stays that way. I'll bet he's chewing Weyburn's ear off, trying to talk his way out."

"I just hope Weyburn doesn't let him go. I hope he stays in jail."

"I hope so too. Mostly for Till's sake."

"What do you mean?"

"Wyeth threatened Till. It may have just been big talk, but you can't ever be sure. If he gets out, keep your eyes peeled. Watch out for Till, for he might not have the clearheadedness to watch out for himself."

"Weyburn!" Cutter Wyeth yelled through the bars as loudly as he could. The man in the next cell, badly hung over, groaned and put his hands over his ears. "Get back here, now!" Wyeth boomed out.

David Weyburn wore an angry scowl as he came out of his anterior office. "Wyeth, I'm tired of your yelling," he said. "What do you want now?"

"I want to know how long I have to put up with being locked up like common scum!"

"You're a thief, Wyeth, and thieves stay locked up a long time," Weyburn said loudly, turning his head a little to make sure Wyeth's hung-over jailed companion heard. Then he drew close to Wyeth's cell and whispered, "Watch what you're saying! You think that man can't repeat what he hears once he's on the street?"

"Then toss him out of here!"

Weyburn looked Wyeth up and down, thinking that no matter what business arrangements existed between them, he would never consider Cutter Wyeth a friend. The man was thoroughly unlikable, possessing an ugliness that went deeper than the merely physical.

Wordlessly, Weyburn went to the other cell, opened it, and told its occupant he was free to go. The hung-over man stood slowly, pain scrawled across his face, and left. When Wyeth heard the office door open and close, he immediately cut into Weyburn.

"What the hell is this, Weyburn? Are you going to let me go or not?"

"I've told you already, Wyeth. If I let you go too quickly, it would only confirm suspicions we don't need."

"Till Cooke's suspicions, you mean?"

"Exactly."

"So Till Cooke still makes the decisions in the county sheriff's office? Is that it?"

"Till Cooke is a man of influence among the cattlemen. He's already burned us enough. I'm not about to give him fuel to burn us more."

"What does that mean? You're not letting me go?"

"Of course you'll go. Tonight. You'll overpower Deputy Ellsworth when he brings you your supper and break free. Deputy Ellsworth will give you no resistance. You'll steal a saddled gelding that will be hitched in front of the office. I'll mount a search, and no trace of you will be found."

"I don't like this waiting around. What if Till Cooke and his Old Boys come calling before I get out of here? They'd have me lynched to a telegraph pole, and you couldn't stop them."

"You think they'd walk right up to this office and take out a prisoner? Cooke's not that big a fool."

"Fool or not, he's a thorn in our side. He needs to be got rid of."

Weyburn stuck his finger through the bars into Wyeth's face. "You don't go getting any ideas about killing Till Cooke. You start taking that kind of risk, and it'll all come crashing down around our ears."

"I ain't worried. You're the sheriff, ain't you? What can they do to you?"

"I'll not argue with you about this, Cutter. You just mind your own affairs, lay low for a while, and for God's sake don't let anybody catch you again. If they bring you back to me, there'd be no way to let you 'escape' again and have anybody believe it was really an escape. Get out of the area awhile, and let me handle Till Cooke. There's better ways than a bullet to deal with some situations."

"Not that I've found," Wyeth muttered.

"If you can't kill a scratching cat, the next best thing is to take out its claws," Weyburn said. "Till Cooke is ripe to be ruined. One good scandal and we could bring him down. He's got that pretty niece of his living right there with him in his own house. A few stories started in the right places, among the right people, and we could scandalize his name so that nobody would so much as let him spit in their yard, much less let him lead them."

Wyeth was not a subtle thinker. What he achieved he achieved in a direct and brutal fashion. "I say let's kill him and be done with it," he said.

"I'm warning you, Cutter: Stay away from Till Cooke. You go after him, and before you can turn around, he'll be after you in turn, and he might just drag me down with him along the way."

Wyeth said nothing more. Weyburn studied him with concern, wondering if he would heed his warning. With Cutter Wyeth there was no telling. Weyburn wished he didn't have to let Wyeth go free. While Wyeth was locked up, he was under control. But keeping him here was impossible. They were partners, after all. And Wyeth could hardly do his part while in a cell. Of course, once Wyeth was out, it would be a challenge indeed to convince men such as Till Cooke that the escape was not his doing.

"Tonight, Cutter," Weyburn said. "Be patient until then."

He returned to his office. Cutter Wyeth swore and began pacing the little cell, back and forth, back and forth, like a panther in a cage.

David Weyburn sat down at his desk and took a series of deep breaths. Sweat broke out on his brow as a surge of unfocused panic passed through him. It was all he could do to keep from leaping up and running out onto the street, yelling.

After a few moments the attack of panic ended and he relaxed. Since taking office, such attacks had come to him from time to time, without warning. They frightened him, for he couldn't ascertain their origin.

Through his mind raced a boyhood memory: his grandfather, raging and fighting in a room behind a barred door in a place where they locked away people who had lost their sanity.

Weyburn thought: Could it be happening to me?

No, no. He refused to accept that. He was just wrought up, that was all. He had so many secrets to hide. Sometimes he felt like a juggler in one of those traveling snake oil shows, trying to keep everything up in the air and fearing that one slip that would bring it all crashing down.

As soon as his deputy Ellsworth arrived, Weyburn

left and headed home. He needed a drink, and the love and companionship of his beloved Magart. The mere thought of her brought him joy and comfort.

As long as he had Magart, everything would be all right.

16

Maria Cruz was an ample woman; it required two towels for her to get fully dry after her baths. For years she had bathed habitually about once every week in room-temperature water, believing anything hotter and more frequent was injurious to health. But lately she had begun to bathe twice weekly, and today's bath was the third of the week.

Yet she still felt dirty, the kind of dirty that didn't go away, no matter how many times she washed. She brushed away the water in her eyes. Most of it had not come from the tin washtub she stood in.

Continuing to wipe away tears, she dressed herself in her nightgown, a long cotton frock given to her by her husband. She wouldn't let herself cry aloud for fear Eduardo would hear her. At the moment he was upstairs, taking his shift at keeping the Lady company. The Lady. That was how Maria thought of her now. She knew that David Weyburn preferred that she be called Mrs. Weyburn, but Maria hadn't been able to do that. No matter what Weyburn said, the Lady wasn't his wife just because she shared his house and bed. She wasn't anybody's wife at all, now that her husband had died in that fire. If she was Mrs. anyone, it was Mrs. Broadmore.

Of course, Maria dared not call her by that name in this house. To do so would invite the fury of David Weyburn. He had despised Folly Broadmore in life, even as he had loved Broadmore's woman. And so, for Maria, she was and would remain simply, the Lady.

When she was dressed, Maria sat down at the little dressing table that Weyburn had given her two years ago as a show of his gratitude for the loyal service she and Eduardo had given him. It had been a wonderful gift, highly prized by her. Yet now even the dressing table could not delight her as it once had. It was tainted by its very association with David Weyburn. David Weyburn the fraud, the thief . . . the murderer.

The latter fact was the part that Maria couldn't bear. She had known for years that her employer was not honest, not the good man he pretended to be. And she hadn't much cared. She herself had been no angel throughout her earlier life; she could hardly condemn her employer for being dishonest when she had been far worse herself. But murder . . . that was a different matter. She could overlook a multitude of David Weyburn's sins, but try as she might, she couldn't bear the knowledge that he had killed Folly Broadmore, then burned his house down around him to destroy the body and cover the evidence of how Broadmore had really died. Eduardo had told her that it wasn't as bad as it sounded. Folly Broadmore had beaten Magart so severely that her brain had been damaged; that was why she was now so childlike. So he had deserved to die, according to Eduardo.

If only Eduardo hadn't told me about it all, Maria thought. *If only he had kept it to himself . . . then I wouldn't have to bear the weight of it on my soul. I wouldn't feel so dirty all the time.*

When she was honest with herself, Maria could not really blame Eduardo for having told her. After all, she had pushed him to it. Knowing something significant and secret had happened between Weyburn and the

Broadmores, she had harangued Eduardo into telling her. Now she regretted it, for what he had revealed was a crushing burden on her soul.

The worst part was the poor Tonkawa woman Floyd Fells had killed. She was the truly innocent victim in this scandal. Fells had dressed the woman's corpse in some of Magart Keller's clothing, and put her alongside the body of Folly Broadmore before the house was set ablaze. And so everyone had believed that Magart Broadmore had died along with her husband. No one dreamed she was still alive and living in the house of David Weyburn, where Weyburn intended she should stay for perpetuity.

It was so foolish, and so impossible! Maria knew that such a house of cards could not stand. Only Weyburn's fierce love for Magart Broadmore kept him under the delusion that she could be hidden from the world forever. Only a handful of people knew about the woman in Weyburn's upper room: Weyburn himself; his ranch manager and associate, Floyd Fells; Eduardo and Maria. And Paco, the poor old fellow who used to come around begging at the ranches. Maria had told him the entire story, simply to unload the weight of it. What harm could have come from telling him? He was harmless and simple, and probably hadn't even understood it.

But since then, Paco hadn't come around, and Maria wondered why.

She knelt beside her bed and took up her rosary. It seemed an alien thing in her hands. Closing her eyes, she tried to pray and could not. How could one as guilty as she send up any kind of prayer and expect to be heard? The very idea was sacrilege.

She was a woman living in secret sin, the sin of helping hide a murder. Every day that she and Eduardo helped perpetuate Weyburn's secret, keeping their silence, her guilt only grew. Surely she would pay the divine penalty for this sin, and Eduardo too. She felt she should confess it, not only to a priest, but also to the law . . . but now the law was Weyburn. And even if she told someone else—the commander at Fort Cade, or the former sheriff, Till Cooke—what would become of her? Would she and Eduardo not both be liable for the parts they had already played in this matter?

She put away the rosary and crawled into bed. There she huddled silently, still weeping, until Eduardo came to join her. He undressed without words and crawled in beside her.

He knew his wife was upset as soon as his hand touched her tight and tense shoulders.

"What is wrong with you, Maria? Are you crying again?"

"No, Eduardo, I . . . yes. Yes, I am crying. I cry every night. I cry as we will both cry in eternal Hell for the sin we are committing."

Eduardo sat up and made her roll to face him. "Hear me, wife: You must not think like this. Don't even think of confession. If the truth came out, we would be punished for what we have done."

"Yes . . . I know that. But I can't carry this weight forever. It crushes me"—she thumped her large and sagging bosom—"here . . . I can feel the weight of it, like a stone."

"We are only being faithful servants. Señor Weyburn has been good to us through many years, Maria."

"But Señor Weyburn is a murderer."

"He killed a man who would have beaten an innocent woman into her grave . . . and he did not mean to kill him. It was the anger of love that made him do it. Perhaps, in God's eyes, that isn't murder."

"Yes, it is murder, and even if it wasn't, what of the Indian woman? The poor Tonkawa?"

"She was only an Indian, Maria."

"If we were killed, there are those who would say of us, 'They were only Mexicans.' Only an Indian? She was a woman made by God's hands, and he will surely smite us down for helping hide her death."

"Keep your voice low, Maria! What if he should hear you? He might fear you will talk, and then—"

"It's too late. I've already told someone."

"Mother of God!"

"It's true—I told the story to Paco."

"Paco—the old thief and beggar?"

"Yes. I couldn't bear to not talk of it, Eduardo. It was a fire inside me. I chose him because he was simple and couldn't understand."

Eduardo took a deep breath. "Maria, Paco is gone. He has been gone for a long time. In town they say he claimed to know a secret about the Broadmore fire. No one believed him . . . but now he is gone, and no one knows where."

"Oh, Eduardo . . ."

"Paco understood what you told him, Maria. It was you who was the fool, the simple one. Not Paco."

"If he is gone, then he is dead, Eduardo! He must be! Señor Weyburn and Señor Fells, they have killed him! Oh, God forgive me!"

"Hush, woman! If they have killed him, then at least we are safe. You were a fool to talk to Paco about what I told you. Because of you, we might have been discovered."

"My husband, is that all you can think of, what would happen to us? Have you no pity for those who have died? Have you no fear of the sin that has been done?"

"I cannot bear the thought of being imprisoned, Maria. And hanging—that would be even worse."

"And what about the sufferings of Hell? Have you no fear of that?"

"Go to sleep, Maria. We will talk no more of this."

They turned their backs on each other. Maria cried for a long time, keeping her sobs silent. As for Eduardo, he simply stared into the darkness.

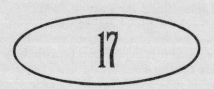

17

"Three head a month?" Weyburn asked, scratching his chin and leaning back in his chair. He was in his office, and across the desk from him sat Floyd Fells, holding a document that bore the imprints of the U.S. Army and Fort Cade. "I see no problem in meeting that demand."

"Neither do I." Fells dropped his voice. "And seldom, I think, will it be necessary to even touch our own herd. We can easily cut three beeves a month out of neighboring herds, dispose of the hides to hide the brands, and deliver the meat to Fort Cade without lifting any eyebrows."

"Yes, but be careful," Weyburn replied. "There's Till Cooke and his ilk already breathing down my neck. They'll be looking for anything they can find against me. Now that I've let Wyeth make his escape, there will be trouble enough for us."

"It would be convenient if our former sheriff met with an accident, don't you think?" Fells ventured.

Weyburn jerked forward, pounding the bottom of his fist on the desktop. "No! You're talking like Wyeth now. There's already been enough killing, and it doesn't sit easily with me. There are lines I don't like to cross."

"Yes," Fells said coldly. "I know."

"Don't worry about Cooke. I have a plan to discredit him in the public eye. Now, let me see that contract."

Fells handed the paper to Weyburn, who studied it for a minute, then signed. He had just handed it back to Fells when the front door burst open and Jed Keller stomped in. Ignoring Fells, he went straight to the side of Weyburn's desk, leaned over on his palms and looked the sheriff in the face.

"I hear that Cutter Wyeth escaped this jail last night."

"Yes. He overpowered one of my deputies and forced his way out. Believe me, I regret it deeply."

"I'm sure you do, Sheriff Weyburn," Keller said mockingly. "Overpowered your deputy, you say? There's no reason for that ever to happen. I know a little about the jail business, you know. A properly trained deputy never puts himself in a position to be overpowered by a prisoner."

Weyburn's eyes flicked to Fells. "Floyd, perhaps you should go now."

Fells stood, looking at Keller like the man had just tangled with a skunk and neglected to clean himself. "Later, David." He waved the contract. "I'll go deliver this paper."

"Weyburn, you and I both know that Cutter Wyeth didn't escape from this jail. You let him walk out."

"That's a serious charge to bring against a legally elected peace officer. Do you have any evidence to support it?"

Keller hesitated. "No," he said. "But sometimes a man knows what he can't prove."

"That carries no weight in a court of law . . . if it's your plan to go that route."

"I have no plan. But there are others who might not be so lenient. And they don't require the kind of proof a court demands."

"You're talking about the so-called Old Boys, I take it? You're treading thin ice, Keller. I might take that comment as a threat."

"I'm not one of the Old Boys, Weyburn. I don't control them, if they even exist. This is no threat, but a warning. You're going to have to prove yourself honest, or you'll start an avalanche that will crush you. I went to the wall for you when I argued to let you take custody of Wyeth. You could have vindicated yourself. You didn't. You let him go free."

"I told you—he escaped."

"Then why are you here? Why aren't you out looking for him?"

"I have a sizable force of deputies doing that as we speak."

"Deputies? The deputies you hired are no more than a gang of trash who've spent more time occupying jail cells than tending them. You're a fool, Weyburn, and you're tying your own noose, one twist at a time."

Weyburn stood and walked to the stove, where he poured himself a cup of coffee. Returning to his desk, he sat down and began drinking, looking Keller up and down. "You know, Jed Keller, there's something about you that I like, and God only knows I can't say what it is. No, no, that's not true. It's because Magart Broadmore was your sister. I look in your face, and I see her. She was a fine woman, and for the sake of your kinship to her, I want to see good things come to you. But you make it hard for me to be so charitable when you act like this. Just let it go, Keller. Leave me to my business, and mind your own."

"Cade is my home now, Weyburn. I have a life here, and an investment. All I want is a peaceful existence and an honest trade in the cattle business. You and your ilk are threatening both." He paused; it was on the tip of his tongue to present to Weyburn his troubling questions about Magart's death and the way that Weyburn seemed somehow connected to it. He didn't get the chance to ask, however, for right then the door opened again and Till Cooke entered, his face as grim as a thunderhead about to burst.

"Weyburn!" Cooke shouted. "Weyburn, you did it, didn't you! You let Wyeth go free!" Cooke wheeled toward Keller. "And you're as much at fault as he is. If you'd let us take Wyeth on to Fort Cade, this wouldn't have happened!"

"Calm down, Cooke," Weyburn said. He was trying to sound composed, but Keller detected a tremble in his voice. Weyburn, he realized, was truly afraid of Till Cooke. He could hardly blame him.

"Calm down? I'll tell you when I'll calm down, you maggot! I'll calm down when you're out of office and in a cell, where you belong. Or perhaps when you're swinging from a mesquite tree somewhere outside town! And don't think that can't happen!"

"Till!" Keller cut in. "You watch your mouth, or you'll say something that you'll later regret."

Cooke shot back, "Are you working for Weyburn now, Jed? Lord knows you seem to take his side of things enough!"

Weyburn was getting mad. "Mr. Cooke, you've just threatened the life of the duly elected sheriff of this county. I could jail you for that."

"You try it, you foul little swine! I'll knock your head down your throat and pull it out your bung!"

"Mr. Cooke, I'm putting you under arrest!"

"Come and get me, then, if you think you're man enough!"

Weyburn moved as if to come around from behind the desk, but then he faltered. The fear on his face couldn't be hidden. Keller saw Weyburn's eye drift down toward his desk drawer and saw his hand twitch restlessly. He knew then that there was a pistol in the drawer, and that Weyburn was thinking of getting it out. And he also knew what would happen if he did: Till

Cooke would draw his own Colt and kill Weyburn where he stood. Keller had to intervene.

"Sheriff, I apologize for my friend here," Keller said, deliberately grasping Cooke's gun arm. Cooke tried to shake him off, but Keller hung on. "Don't arrest him, please. I'll get him out of here and talk sense into him. Just let it be. It would be best for all of us."

Weyburn glared at Cooke, his lip trembling. Then he nodded curtly.

"Come on, Till," Keller said.

"Let go of me, Jed."

"Till, I'll not see you hang or spend the rest of your days locked away for murder. Think of Claire, if nothing else. Come on. Let's get out of here before things get worse."

Till Cooke, still staring at Weyburn, jerked his arm free. But he did not draw his pistol. "All right," he said. "I'll leave. But hear me, Weyburn! The cattlemen are getting sore weary of you. They know what you are. If Cutter Wyeth is found by any of them, you won't have a chance to lock him up again. All you'll be able to do with him is deliver him to the coroner."

"That's a threat of murder, Mr. Cooke. I won't forget you made it."

"I hope you won't. And while you're remembering that, remember this too: A noose can choke the life out of a crooked sheriff as easy as out of an outlaw like Wyeth. You think on that, Weyburn. Think on it when you lie down at night. And from now on, you might want to make sure your pistol is always on your hip, instead of in your desk. You might be called on to use it."

Cooke wheeled and went out the door. Keller followed. At the door he glanced back to see Weyburn, white-faced, sink back down into his chair. He looked like a man who had just heard a judge sentence him to death . . . and that, Keller realized with a chill, was not far from what had just happened.

Cooke was mounting his horse at a hitch post two buildings down when Keller caught up with him. "Till, you just made a bad mistake," he said. "If anything happens now that remotely looks like vigilante revenge, Weyburn's going to come straight to your door."

"Let him come," Cooke said. "I'd welcome the opportunity to settle with him, man to man."

"Don't be a fool, Till."

Cooke looked down at Keller from the saddle. "I'd rather be a fool than a traitor and a coward, Jed." And then he rode off, spurring his horse to a gallop, which drew much attention from those on the street.

It was clear that Cooke had intended his last words to sting Keller, and he had succeeded. Keller watched Cooke ride away, and wished he had never come to Cade at all.

When Eduardo Cruz went to his bedroom in David Weyburn's big stone house that night, he found Maria crying again.

His voice was cold. "Why are you crying now?"

Maria dabbed her eyes. "I am crying because now it is worse than before," she said.

"How? What has happened?"

"I was with the Lady all day today," Maria said. "I should have seen it earlier . . . but it was only today that I realized it."

"What?"

Maria put her arms around her husband and began weeping again. Through her crying she said, "There is another one now that will surely suffer when all this ends. An innocent one."

"Who do you speak of?"

Maria looked into her husband's eyes. "The Lady is pregnant, Eduardo. She has been pregnant for a long time now, and I've been blind to it. She is carrying his child, Señor Weyburn's child, and she is too much a child herself to even know it. And what will become of it when it is born? How will an innocent child fail to suffer, born into this house of sin?"

She began to sob loudly, and nothing Eduardo could do would comfort her.

18

For three days there was a tense lull, and then the time of vengeance began and the word went out up and down the Brazos: The Old Boys are back.

The first to fall victim was a man named Vincent Calvin, a stock thief who had been driven from Cade during the earlier days of the Old Boys, but who had returned at the first of the year and stolen horses both from ranchers and a small settlement of Tonkawas. His body was found hanging from a mesquite tree a mile north of Cade, and around his neck was a hand-lettered sign that said, *Justice*.

The incident generated great excitement up and down the Brazos. Keller walked the streets of Cade and heard nothing but talk about the hanging. "The Old Boys are stringing up the criminals again," people would say. "There'll be plenty more no-accounts who taste their justice before it's done."

Sure that Till Cooke was leading the Old Boys, and fearing he would be immediately arrested for it, Keller rode to his house. He hadn't seen Cooke since the encounter in Weyburn's office, and didn't know if he would even be allowed on Cooke's property.

Claire was there alone. "Weyburn sent deputies to

115

talk to Uncle Till," she told Keller. "But they didn't arrest him, because he was able to prove he had been in a saloon in Cade at the time the hanging happened."

"He really was in that saloon?"

"Absolutely. There were several witnesses."

Keller was surprised, and mystified. "Then who led the Old Boys, I wonder?"

"I don't know, but it wasn't Uncle Till—thank God."

"Amen to that, Claire. Where is he now?"

"Out somewhere on the ranch. He'll be back soon."

Keller said, "Maybe I shouldn't be here when he returns."

Claire nodded sadly. "Maybe you shouldn't."

That same day in Cade, Sheriff David Weyburn issued a public proclamation: Vigilante activity would not be tolerated, and any members of the so-called Old Boys would be prosecuted to the fullest extent of the law.

The people of Cade were divided on the issue of the proclamation. Some, aware of the cattlemen's mounting suspicions of their sheriff, and believing that Cutter Wyeth's escape from Weyburn's custody had been no accident, declared that Weyburn was simply scared of the Old Boys, fearing their noose would find his own neck. Others, mostly those who had not been in Cade back in the days when the Old Boys first rode, agreed with the proclamation and said vigilantes were worse than those they persecuted.

Two nights later the Old Boys struck again. This time they hanged two men in an old stable right on the edge of Cade. Both were suspected horse thieves, and one was said to have ridden with the Wyeths. Keller was in Cade when these two bodies were brought in, and he recognized one as the man who had hidden behind the creek bank during the gun battle.

The next day, Weyburn issued another proclamation, even more sternly worded than before, and included a thousand dollar reward on behalf of the county for information leading to the arrest and conviction of any of the Old Boys. The sheriff's detractors laughed loudly at this new declaration, and whispered among themselves that some of the county solons who had approved the reward were most likely Old Boys themselves.

Once again a visit was paid to Till Cooke, and once again he had a clear alibi. He had attended a "singing" at the local church, in clear view of three-score congregation members, at the time of the lynchings. This word brought amusement in Cade, for everyone knew that Till Cooke hadn't attended church in years up until that particular night.

Keller continued to be mystified. If Till Cooke was behind the revival of the Old Boys, he was certainly handling himself carefully, and taking no direct part in the lynchings. Perhaps he wasn't involved at all; perhaps others had actually taken up the gauntlet in his place.

Keller hoped that was true, and quietly investigated to see if he could determine who was leading the mysterious nocturnal lynch mob. He asked Charlie Lilly to make similar investigations, knowing that Lilly was more knowledgeable than he of the subtle workings of life around Cade. Keller was unable to find even a hint of who made up this new incarnation of the Old Boys, and Lilly reported no better luck.

After the double lynching, everything was quiet for two weeks. Talk about the Old Boys subsided, and life began to seem more normal again. There were a few noticeable differences; the streets of Cade were quieter than ever before, and horse theft declined, even though it did not vanish. Suspected stock thieves who had openly showed themselves in the saloons and dance halls of the town were now conspicuously hard to find.

Weyburn continued to search for the vigilantes, and even persuaded the commander at Fort Cade to send out a party of soldiers to patrol the county nightly in search of any lynch mobs. After a week the searches were discontinued, and the general wisdom had it that the military leadership of Fort Cade actually supported the Old Boys' efforts, and had agreed to Weyburn's request primarily as a token favor based on his contract to deliver three beeves a day to the fort to feed the soldiers.

That contract itself was a point of discussion among the cattlemen who were already suspicious of Weyburn. Since the beef deliveries had begun, the cattlemen had quietly watched their own herds, and Weyburn's, and it was noted by some that Weyburn's stock didn't seem to decrease at the rate his delivery schedule would indicate. Yet cattle from other herds continually declined. Might the sheriff, through Floyd Fells, be raiding his neighbors' holdings to fulfill his contract at no expense to himself?

Till Cooke was at the lead of those cattlemen who spread that suspicion. Keller kept close watch on his old friend, who was growing quite reckless in his willingness to publicly slander Weyburn. Cooke's escape from official linkage with the Old Boys had made him rather cavalier and mocking, and on three occasions he shouted at Weyburn himself on the streets of Cade, taunting his inability to halt the vigilante activity. He also voiced his own suspicions about how Weyburn was fulfilling his contract with the Army. Before long the animosity between the former and current sheriff became a source of great entertainment all over the county.

And then the animosity took on a darker aspect, one that hit Till Cooke like a hammer. Rumors began circulating that Cooke's relationship with his niece was not innocent. Whispers of scandal rode on the undercurrents. Till Cooke was so stung and surprised that he took ill to his bed.

Keller was just as angry, and confronted Weyburn. The sheriff denied any part in the rumors, but Keller didn't believe him.

It was the beginning of a great change of attitude for Jed Keller. So far, he had managed to remain a relatively stable force in the tense atmosphere around Cade. But now Claire, the woman he had come to love, was being slandered. He could no longer stand by.

But what could he do? How could he fight something as intangible as a rumor? He knew Weyburn was behind it all, yet there was not a thing he could do to prove it or combat its effects.

Keller began to feel like a man standing on the edge of a windy precipice, barely able to hang on.

Time passed, and the Old Boys rode several times again. Each time there was no forewarning, no sightings of mysterious riders in the night, and—seemingly—no one who had any idea who comprised the vigilante group. Each night after they had ridden, only one piece of evidence would remain: a fresh corpse or two swinging from mesquite branches, telegraph poles, or barn rafters, and on each a sign bearing the word that was the Old Boys' signature: *Justice*.

And each time, Till Cooke had an alibi. Keller was completely stumped, and wished he could ask Cooke about it. That, however, was out of the question. As weeks rolled into months, Till Cooke remained angry at Jed Keller for what had passed between them.

His estrangement from Cooke was a sad thing for Jed Keller. It also made it difficult to carry on his growing romance with Claire O'Keefe. At first he tried to avoid calling on her when he knew Cooke was home, until finally that became too inconvenient, and he began going to see her whenever he felt like it. She would always meet him in the yard, and whenever Cooke was home, Keller would know it by the slamming of the shutters.

19

Calvin McBrearty, district attorney, was a strapping fellow, broad of face and body, with an overflow of unkempt white hair and a pale mustache that was well-groomed, pampered, and much admired by its owner. McBrearty was a clearheaded man who lived under only one significant delusion: that his flourishing facial ornament was greatly admired by the local female population. Everyone knew his conviction and laughed up his sleeve about it, and many a woman deliberately stared at McBrearty's mustache when he passed her on the boardwalk, just to keep his delusion alive for its entertainment value.

Another well-known fact about McBrearty related to his love of courtroom battle, the bloodier the better. He prided himself on his ability to maintain a poker face in the midst of debate, never revealing by any flick of the brow or twitch of the lip, whether he perceived himself to be losing or winning. But unbeknownst to him, the mustache provided a public barometer of his thoughts. When the case was going his way he would stroke that mustache lovingly. When the defense was showing up better than his prosecution, however, he would tug on the left side of the mustache. "He's the first man I ever met whose mind could be read in his nose hair," Till Cooke had once commented to his friends.

Keller, still haunted by suspicions that his sister's death had something to do with David Weyburn, and remembering that Cooke had asked the district attorney to investigate Weyburn's past, called on McBrearty one bright Wednesday afternoon. He wondered if McBrearty would even be willing to talk to him, since he had come to ask for information he wasn't legally entitled to. Keller was pleased when the prosecutor welcomed him openly, saying he had heard of him and knew him to be a good man. When McBrearty heard Keller's question, however, his hand drifted to the mustache; Keller noted he tugged instead of stroked, and took that as a bad portent.

"The truth is, Mr. Keller, that it violates the policy of this office for me to comment to a member of the public about the nature or results of any investigation," McBrearty said. "As a matter of fact, I'm not actually at liberty even to state an investigation is taking place." A long pause, and then he stroked rather than pulled. "In this case, however, I'm inclined to talk to you not as district attorney to citizen, but as man to man. I know that Till Cooke has certainly told you that he asked me to investigate Weyburn, so I see no cause to hide that from you. Come on—let me buy you a beer, and I'll tell you what I can about our good sheriff. Of course, if you ever reveal I spoke to you about this, I'll deny it and find some pretext or another to make your life a legal hell for a good spell. Will you buy those terms?"

"I'll buy them. I want to know what you know about David Weyburn."

They crossed the street to the nearest saloon, and McBrearty signaled for two beers. They sat at a back table, where they could talk without being heard. McBrearty drank half of his beer before he began speaking.

"Sheriff David Weyburn has a background that is as checkered as this tablecloth," McBrearty said through his napkin, with which he lightly dabbed beer foam off his well-waxed facial treasure. "He's faced a variety of charges in a variety of places. Only one ever stuck to him, and that was a charge of stealing two cattle from a neighbor when he was twenty years old. Through the kindness of the victim, he was let off with payment for the cattle, plus a modest fine.

"It's the charges that never were proven that concern me. David Weyburn, who has also gone by the name of Daniel Weyburn, David Way, and William Burns, has been accused of everything from rustling to embezzlement. The man was born in Georgia, lost his father, a shopkeeper, when he was twelve, and his mother when he was fifteen. After her death, he left Georgia, headed first into Illinois, where he supposedly was run out of one town for stealing bread from a bakery shelf not once, but three times. His movements after that I can't trace, but it seems he wound up in eastern Colorado, working on a ranch, and from there came to Texas. While in Colorado he was accused of rustling for his employer, but his superior apparently got him out of trouble by agreeing to pay a heavy fine on his behalf in lieu of prosecution. Why he did this is hard to understand until you learn that Weyburn was later accused of blackmailing his employer. Suffice it to say he came away from Colorado a relatively well-off young man.

"He came to Texas after that and operated a ranch near the Arkansas border, where he apparently did quite well until he abruptly sold out and moved in our direction. My counterpart in Weyburn's former county tells me Weyburn was more or less driven out. The accusation was horse theft, and he came nigh getting himself lynched."

"I would think that would give him a decent respect for vigilantes," Keller said.

"I'm sure it has," McBrearty replied. "Though

from what I hear these days, Weyburn may well not have been scared enough to change his ways."

"There's one thing I can't figure," Keller said. "That big stone house of his, two hired servants, fine ranch land—you're saying he got money enough for all that through blackmail and stock theft?"

"No. Most of his money came from his wife. He inherited it when she died."

"Weyburn was married?"

"Yes. Most people here know he was married once, and that his wife died. In fact, he was married twice. He married his first wife five years ago; she died the year after. Through an earlier inheritance out of New York, she was quite a wealthy woman, several years older than Weyburn."

"How did she die?"

"In childbirth. She was too old for it, I guess. The child died as well. Weyburn apparently took his wife's death badly. He married soon after that, out of grief and loneliness, I suppose. That marriage didn't last a year."

"Divorce?"

"No. Weyburn attempted to obtain one, but his wife wouldn't grant it."

"So he's still married?"

"Legally, yes. But he lives alone, except for two servants, who have been with him since his first marriage. Two Mexicans, a married couple named Cruz."

Keller said, "Mr. McBrearty, let me ask you something. Have you heard any whispers that there might have been something, say, unusual about the fire that killed my sister and her husband?"

"No . . . well, wait a moment. I did hear that Paco the Mex had made a comment or two to that effect —but nobody ever believed Paco. He was a known liar. Full of fantasies."

"And now he's gone."

"Mr. Keller, do you know something about Weyburn that you should tell me?"

Keller fixed his eyes on his beer and pursed his lips. Then he shook his head. "Nothing substantial . . . nothing but feelings, really. But maybe I'll know more soon."

"If you do, you tell me." McBrearty shifted the subject. "Mr. Keller, as a man of the cattle business, do you know anything about the current vigilante activity?"

Keller grinned. "If you're asking me if I'm one of the Old Boys, I can truthfully tell you I'm not."

"Good. And I hope you'll stay out of such affairs. They aren't legal, you know." He glanced from side to side before continuing. "Though I admit, the Old Boys are certainly efficient, and they target just the right people. They achieve the same ends I seek, but without the legal mumbo-jumbo I'm bound to follow. Now, my friend, I must say good day. I seem to stay endlessly busy of late."

Keller stayed at the table alone for several minutes after the district attorney left, not sure why he had stopped short of revealing that Paco had been afraid of Floyd Fells and had vanished the very day Fells had seen him and the Mexican talking in the alley. Perhaps he would tell McBrearty about it . . . but not today. It wasn't yet time for that; he needed to know more.

When he left the saloon, Weyburn was standing on the other side of the street, looking in his direction. Both men stared at each other, and Weyburn turned away.

I'll bet he saw McBrearty leaving too, Keller thought. *I wonder if he figured out we were talking? If he did, I'll bet he's sweating.*

The thought made him smile. He waved at Weyburn and strode off whistling as the sheriff glowered and turned away.

20

The hour was eleven at night, the wind was up, and Till Cooke had just sat up in bed, roused by something he had heard in his sleep, but which had vanished like a dream upon awakening.

"Claire?" he called, sitting up in bed. "Have you come home, Claire?"

Claire was supposed to be away visiting Charlotte Allison, wife of neighboring rancher Hal Allison, and had planned to stay the night. The Allisons were among those who knew better than to believe the vile rumors being spread about Cooke and his niece—rumors Cooke was convinced originated with David Weyburn. Charlotte Allison's invitation for Claire to visit had been issued out of kindness, to give Claire a chance to get away from home for a time and enjoy some diversion. Being home around her brooding uncle seemed hard on Claire these days.

"Claire?" Cooke called again, swinging his feet off the side of the bed. White legs sticking out from beneath the tail of his nightshirt, Cooke stood and left his tiny bedroom. It was dark outside, but enough light remained to illuminate the little house.

Then he heard a noise and realized that this was

what had penetrated his sleep. It was the nicker of a horse, and not one of his own, if he judged the sound rightly.

He rubbed his stubbled chin, slipped back into his bedroom and pulled on his trousers. He stuck his bare feet into his boots, then crouched. From beneath the bed he pulled a long wooden box that contained a maple-stocked twelve-gauge shotgun, already loaded.

The horse made another noise; it was closer now. Cooke left the bedroom and went through the house to the window. He peered around the corner of it.

A rider was outside, though at first he looked not so much like a man as a sack of grain heaped onto a saddled horse. Cooke heard a groan. "By heaven, that man's hurt!" Cooke muttered.

He couldn't see the man's face, for his head was down and crowned by a broad-brimmed hat. Cooke shifted the shotgun to his left hand, opened the door and went out.

"I'm Till Cooke, mister—you shot or something?"

A groan, filled with pain.

"What's wrong with you?"

"Help me . . ." Cooke couldn't recognize the whispering, raspy voice.

"Hold on, I'm coming. We'll get you down from there and see just what—"

The man straightened suddenly, and moonlight bathed his face. "Howdy, Till Cooke," Cutter Wyeth said, grinning. "How are you this fine evening?" Then he shot him through the center of the chest.

"That's for trying to get me hung," Wyeth said, swinging his smoking pistol upright. "I told you I wouldn't forget it."

"Wyeth . . ." Cooke had dropped his shotgun when he fell. Now he groped for it, his hand straining toward it. Wyeth lowered his pistol again and shot Cooke through the arm. The groping hand went limp.

"You're a stubborn old squat, Cooke, that much I'll

say for you. Now tell me, old man, where's that pretty
niece of yours? Inside?"

"I'll kill you, Wyeth, kill you . . ."

"No," Wyeth calmly said. "It's me who's doing the
killing tonight—remember?" He shot a third time, striking Cooke in the forehead and killing him instantly.

Wyeth dismounted, keeping his pistol out in case
Cooke's niece showed up in the door with a gun. He
toed Cooke's body. Satisfied Cooke was dead, Wyeth
stepped over him and entered the house. He came out
again a minute later, disappointed to have found no female inside. Too bad. Had she been home, he could
have made his revenge against Till Cooke all the more
complete, and all the more personally gratifying.

Cutter Wyeth holstered his pistol and mounted.
Looking down one last time at Cooke's body, he
grinned. "Hope that when they find you, the buzzards
have left enough to bury, old man." He headed for his
horse, then paused a moment. Stooping, he picked up
Cooke's shotgun. A fine weapon, costly and well-kept,
and for him a meaningful souvenir.

Hefting up the shotgun, he mounted and rode off
into the darkness.

Jed Keller longed to comfort Claire O'Keefe, but
didn't know how. What comfort could he give another
when he had none himself? Till Cooke . . . dead, murdered. It was inconceivable. When he had first heard it,
Keller became sick to his stomach.

Now he stood beside Claire on a windy hillside,
listening numbly as a final psalm was read before Till
Cooke's body was given back to the earth. Keller was an
inwardly severed man at the moment. One part of him
was a grieving human being, emotional and consumed
by the realization that an old friend was forever gone.
The other part, the lawman portion that would not die
no matter how much Keller tried to kill it, was cold and

rational and busily engaged in an evaluation of Cooke's murder. Who had shot him, and why?

Might it have been Weyburn or one of his deputies? Weyburn certainly bore enough hatred of Cooke to make him do it. Perhaps when Weyburn had seen him talking to the district attorney, it had somehow set him off. Yet Keller doubted Weyburn was behind this. For one thing, it didn't seem quite his style, and for another, he had already found his own means of dealing with Cooke: He had destroyed his reputation with rumors. Keller had no question that Weyburn had started the tales about Cooke and Claire. He doubted Weyburn would have felt the need to murder Cooke's physical person as well as his reputation.

As a former sheriff, Cooke was bound to have made enemies. His killer might have been the holder of some old grudge from years past. Or perhaps the grudge had a more recent origin.

If so, Keller had a good idea who the killer was, for he clearly remembered Cutter Wyeth's threat. It racked him with guilt. *It was me who urged that Wyeth be turned over to Weyburn. I knew the odds were good that Weyburn would let him go, but I encouraged it anyway. I was a fool . . . and now Till is murdered.*

After the burying, Keller helped Claire into her buggy, then climbed into the driver's seat. "I don't think you should go back home just yet," he said. "The memory is too fresh."

"No," she said. "Take me back. I'm not running from what happened. I'll not do that."

Cooke's ranch house seemed terribly empty and forlorn when they arrived. Keller tried to steer Claire away from the bloodied spot where her uncle had died, but she would not be led. She walked to the rust-colored stain on the earth and looked sadly down at it.

"Murdered," she said. "That's the part I can't accept. To die naturally is one thing. But to be killed because of someone's hatred . . ." She said no more, ending her thought with a shudder.

"He was a brave man, Claire. I was at his side for many a day, and I know what his mettle was. I'd like to know how whoever it was got the jump on him. He wasn't one to be fooled easy. And why was he out here unarmed? That has me confused. It wasn't like Till to be careless."

Claire frowned thoughtfully. "Wait a minute," she said. She entered the house. Keller, puzzled by what she was up to, rolled a quirly and was just lighting up when she emerged.

"Uncle Till kept his shotgun under his bed," she said. "It's gone."

"Gone!" Keller let smoke drift out through his nostrils. "So he didn't come out here unarmed. He was tricked, or overpowered, and his killer took the shotgun. Is anything else missing?"

"Not that I can tell."

Keller swore. The thought of Cooke's killer making off with that particular gun made him seethe. That was a special gun, one he himself had given Cooke many years ago, at the time he left his service.

"I'm going to find Till's killer, Claire," Keller said. "I'm going to find him, and make sure he pays for what he did."

"Jed, don't get into the middle of this," Claire pleaded. "You can't bring him back—and I'm afraid I'll just lose you too. I couldn't bear it. Leave this to the law to deal with. You yourself have said so many times that you just want to be through with this sort of thing."

"I can't leave this to the law, Claire. Not while the law is David Weyburn."

"Jed, do you think Weyburn might be behind the killing?"

"Maybe . . . perhaps just indirectly, but he could be behind it."

"Indirectly?"

"Yes. I think it may be because of Weyburn that Till's killer was free and able to do this."

It required only a moment for Claire to comprehend the implication. "Cutter Wyeth?"

"Yes. It's just a suspicion, but a strong one. He did threaten Till, after all. And if he did kill him, then that's all the more reason I have to hunt him down. It was me who talked Till into letting Weyburn take custody of Wyeth. And Weyburn, whatever talk about 'escape' he might make, let Wyeth go free. So it's partly my fault Till is dead, Claire. I owe it to him to find his killer. Do you understand?"

"Yes," she said. "I do." Then she came to him, put her arms around him and held him as if she feared never being able to hold him again.

Back home that night, Keller sat up alone, smoking and thinking. He was recalling Till Cooke's words about written law and unwritten law, and his own stubborn rejection of that way of thinking.

Keller had been sure he was right in his own thinking at the beginning. Now nothing seemed sure at all. Perhaps Cooke had known far better than he the depth of wickedness being dealt with when one took on the likes of Cutter Wyeth and David Weyburn. Perhaps the unwritten law that Cooke had believed in was the law of right and wrong, and of good men being free to take a stand against bad ones.

Keller fell asleep at last, still in his chair. He woke himself up crying. Crying—and he hadn't cried in years.

He cried because Till Cooke had died still estranged from him, just as Magart had. It seemed absurd and tragic. And it was too late to do anything about it.

He stood, stretching and yawning. Walking to his window, he looked out over the dawn-lighted land.

It may be too late for me to patch my differences with Till, he thought, *but there are still some things it's not too late to do. And now, for the first time, I'm ready to do them. I never would have thought I would come to it, but I'm ready.*

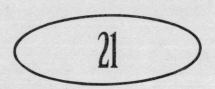

21

For the next forty-eight hours Jed Keller was a man in torment. He ached to find Cooke's killer, but as one man, there was little he could do. Twice he caught himself thinking that since he needed some guidance on how to begin his investigation, he ought to go talk to Till Cooke. Till would know what to do . . . and then Keller remembered the truth, and his pain and distraction grew all the worse.

On the second day after Cooke's burial, clouds began to roll across the sky and the temperature fell several degrees. "Looks like bad weather may be rolling in," Doyle Boston said, studying the sky. "Cattle are restless; look at them. Don't know what to do with themselves."

"I'm restless too," Keller commented. "But I know what I need to do with myself. If the Old Boys were to ride up right now and ask me to join them, I'd be with them in a second."

Darkness fell, and the anticipated storm still had not come, though the threat of it lingered.

Keller was outside, beneath the overhang he had built onto his house, watching the wind rise and whip dust across the yard. He was smoking, though the wind burned up each quirly within a minute of lighting it. Keller's spirits were no brighter, but for some reason he had a sense of ominous anticipation, as if the wind was carrying a hint of something new.

Keller closed his eyes, trying to relax. When he opened them, Charlie Lilly and Doyle Boston were standing before him, dressed to ride.

"Jed, get ready to go," Lilly said.

Keller, puzzled and surprised, opened his mouth to ask why, and where. Before the words were out, Lilly shook his head. "It'll be clear soon enough," he said.

Keller stood and nodded. He understood now, without being told. He retreated inside, then came out again. His Colt was in his gun belt, strapped around his waist, and he carried his Winchester.

He noticed that Doyle Boston had a stout coil of rope over his shoulder. Keller's eyes flicked over to meet Lilly's, and he exchanged his unspoken question for a silent confirmation.

It was a time for decision. What he had said before was mere talk. This was the real thing.

He stood silently and thought about Till's coffin being lowered into the open grave. "I'll saddle up," he said.

"Things look different now than before, eh, Jed?"

"Yes," Keller said. "They do."

They rode through the night as clouds roiled above and distant thunder shook the Brazos country. The smell of the coming storm was strong, and matched the rising fire in Keller's spirit. No more holding out or holding back. No more bowing the head at the altar of old memories. No more conundrums over written and unwritten law, or over surface loyalties and deeper ones. He was where he should be.

They came to the old picket house where the late cattleman Sayler Todd once lived. The light of a small campfire flared in the middle of the old stable yard. Keller, Lilly, and Boston rode up close and stopped.

"Who goes there?"

"Justice by hemp," Lilly replied.

"Come in, then," the voice called back.

Keller could tell by the lack of reaction to his appearance that he was expected tonight. He looked around at nearly a score of faces that were reddened by the firelight. Most of these men he knew. The majority were ranch owners or foremen, and a couple were particularly trusted cowhands. But in addition there was a shopkeeper, a butcher, and even a saloon operator, these three being Cade townsmen.

Keller scanned the group, mentally clicking off the names of those he recognized: Will Cornmiller, Arden Spann, Larry Hite, Hank Kelvin, Irwin Dunbar, Joe Decatur, Levon Hatley, Sheller Calahan, Gunter House, Ben Potts, Manfred Burroughs, Gordy Snow, Bonner Elrod, and others, all of them men of high reputation and known stoutness of heart. Even Hal Allison was here.

"Gentlemen," Keller said, nodding a general greeting.

Nods and mumbles in return, then Lilly went to the side of the fire. "There's no turning back for us now," he said. "The death of Till Cooke shows us there's yet a lot of cleaning up to be done along the Brazos."

"It was Wyeth who done it," Kelvin said.

"We don't know that, Hank," Lilly replied. He paused. "But I believe it too. It was Wyeth. Had to be."

"He's been seen back in the county within the past week," said Arden Spann.

"Maybe we'll find him tonight," Lilly said. "Or maybe not. One thing I know—no, two: We'll find somebody worth the finding tonight, and sooner or later we'll catch up with Wyeth himself. And this time there'll be no men with badges or soldiers in uniforms to get in the way of justice. That right?"

A rumble of assent broke from the group. Then Lilly looked at Keller.

"That right, Jed?"

"That's right," he said.

They found three of them together, camped in a big Sibley tent left over from the previous decade's war. They resisted only a little, for canvas walls gave no protection from bullets, and three against a score was no odds at all.

"Calahan?" Lilly said when the three were lined up, their pale faces tight with fright and illuminated by the light of a pine-tar torch that one of the Old Boys had lighted.

Sheller Calahan, who owned a medium-sized spread bordering the south bank of the Brazos, nudged his horse forward a step. "Them's the three," he said.

Arden Spann, Calahan's ranch boss, came around the other side of the tent, leading a pair of horses. "These are ours," he said. "They got a passel of them inside a rope fence. Gunter, Manfred, Gordy, I seen horses belonging to you in there too. And there's others."

"I don't want to hang!" one of the thieves pleaded.

"Too late to be begging—you could have avoided all this by not stealing our horses to begin with," Calahan said. There was not a trace of sympathy in his voice. He, like the others, had been victimized too long by men such as these, who stole without conscience and gave thought to mercy only when it was they who wanted to receive it.

"At least give us the chance for a trial," one of the others asked. He was more composed than the first, though obviously scared. "Hanging us without a trial ain't fair."

" 'None but the brave deserves the fair,' " Charlie Lilly quoted. "That's John Dryden."

The thieves seemed confused by the quote; one of them loudly denied that any of them were named Dryden. The Old Boys, familiar with Lilly's poetic quotes and citations, laughed, but it was a harsh and serious laughter.

Calahan had a more direct answer for the horse thief's plea for a trial. "There's several hundred of your kind already indicted in this state, and most will never go to trial as it is. Not one stock thief in ten gets caught —unless it's by men who won't stand around waiting for the official law to work. You want a trial? All right, we'll give you one." Calahan looked to his partners. "These men stand charged as thieving scum on the face of Texas. Guilty or not guilty?"

"Guilty!" the cry came back.

Calahan smiled a very fearsome smile. "There you are, men. Fairly tried and fairly convicted."

"Doyle, yonder limb looks stout enough to suffice," Charlie Lilly said to Boston, pointing at a nearby tree.

"Wait," Jed Keller said. Every face turned to him; Lilly gazed at him intently. Was Keller again about to waffle?

Keller dismounted, took the torch from the man holding it, and walked up to the thieves. He looked into the face of the first, who had been maintaining only the most tenuous hold on his emotions. The man began to sob; he sank to his knees, face in hands. Keller moved on to the second man, the one who had pleaded for trial. This man didn't break down, but managed to look Keller in the eye, though falteringly.

"Friend, you've got nothing to gain by refusing to answer my question, for you'll be no more dead after telling me the truth than you'll be after lying. Do you ride with Cutter Wyeth?"

"I have . . . I don't no more."

"You're independent?"

"Yes sir."

"Do you know if it was Cutter Wyeth who killed the former sheriff, Till Cooke?"

"No sir, I don't know who killed him. It sure wasn't me."

Keller moved to the third man, who had said nothing at all. He was thin and had a nose like a hawkbill knife. "What about you? You know who killed Till Cooke?"

"I do."

The forthright and unhesitant answer surprised the entire group. "Who was it, then?"

"Is it worth my freedom for you to know?"

Keller glanced at Lilly, then at the others. In the darkness they were phantom men on phantom mounts. Keller held up the torch to illuminate Lilly's face, for this was Lilly's decision to make, not his.

"They have to hang," Lilly said.

Keller turned back to the man. "You heard that—I can't offer you freedom. But telling the truth is a good thing for a man to do, especially one swing away from his judgment day."

The man swallowed and pulled his lips tight. "It was Wyeth who killed the lawman," he said. "He come back in the county two weeks ago, looking for Nancy Scarlet. I reckon he pined for her. But he also come back to kill Till Cooke. Told me that himself." The man nodded. "Well, I told it. Makes this old dirty soul feel that much cleaner."

Keller turned away and climbed back onto his horse. His heart was hammering, and he sweated like he had just finished a fast run up a steep hill. He knew what would happen now, and that once it had happened, he would undeniably be the very thing he had sworn never to be. A vigilante. An Old Boy. He couldn't back out now. So be it.

Doyle Boston threw his rope over the limb and tied a noose. A couple of others in the group joined him with ropes of their own. The three horse thieves watched the process wordlessly; the first had gotten control of himself and now only whimpered a little. Keller was glad the man had stopped his crying. It was a sorry thing to die like a coward; he couldn't wish that kind of shame even on a horse thief.

Keller didn't want to watch the actual hangings, but he made himself do it. Having come this far, he wouldn't falter at the last minute. When the horses ran out from under the men and the ropes pulled tight, the Old Boys watched in silence until it was clear that death had come.

"Well, that's three more gone," Charlie Lilly said. He glanced from the swinging bodies up into the branches of the hanging tree. " 'Casting the body's vest aside, My soul into the boughs does glide.' Andrew Marvell, 'The Garden.' " He snorted. "Of course, in the case of these three, I suppose the souls are more likely working their way down through the roots than up through the boughs."

Several others chuckled, but Keller couldn't join in. What had just happened was, he believed, the working out of justice, however rough, but to him it was also a somber event. He had made a major transformation tonight, for the sake of Till Cooke's memory, and he hoped it was the right one.

Spann left signs, each bearing the word "Justice," on all three bodies—signs made in advance, with loops already attached so they could be slipped over the victims' heads like medals on chains. This, Keller realized, was a purposeful and efficient group of men.

They rode back home, and Keller fell into his bed, fully clothed, and slept without dreams.

22

Keller went to Lilly's cookhouse the next morning after breakfast. Lilly was cleaning his pots, whistling, and cutting up various beef organs to add to a stew that was already in the works on the stove. A battered book of English poetry was propped open against a flour sack on a shelf, so that Lilly could read as he worked.

Keller helped himself to a cupful of coffee. "Charlie, I never would have guessed you to be the one," he said. "Wouldn't have guessed it in a century."

"Which is precisely why Till Cooke asked me to do it on his behalf," Lilly replied. "Obviously he couldn't do it himself, not with Weyburn's eyes on him—and the eyes of about everybody else too. He might have asked you instead of me . . . had circumstances been different."

"I would've turned him down."

"I know. I guess he knew it too."

"Why did you agree, Charlie? Night-riding doesn't seem to fit my impression of you."

"I believe in justice. And in this county, with Weyburn in office, there's no justice except the kind that's dealt out directly. Nor is there a hand to deal directly but our own."

"I want to get Cutter Wyeth, Charlie. I want to see him brought to justice for murdering Till Cooke."

"So do I."

"So when do we ride again, and look for him?"

"Tomorrow night. And if we don't find him then, another night hence. And so on and so on, until this county is clean again."

Keller took a swallow of the strong coffee. "This county won't be fully clean until David Weyburn is gone. Till Cooke was right about him. He smells like trouble from a mile away, and trouble he'll be as long as he's got power."

Life was different for Jed Keller after he began riding with the Old Boys. For the next two months, hardly a week passed that didn't see Keller, Lilly, Boston, and at least a few of the other Old Boys speeding through the darkness, often with hooves silenced by muffling pads and always with ropes at ready, to leave behind them one, two, sometimes three corpses hanging with signs about their necks. So common did the sight of the bodies become that the people in and around Cade lost their sense of shock upon seeing them hanging limp and white in the morning sunlight. They would cut them down, haul them into town, and turn them over to Sheriff David Weyburn.

Weyburn, everyone noticed, was growing increasingly distressed by his inability to stop the vigilante activity. Some wondered why he even wanted to stop it; by all common sense, it was making his work easier. Unless, folks would whisper, doing the job of a proper sheriff wasn't David Weyburn's true work at all, but only a cover.

Questions abounded. Where did the man's money come from, anyway? And how was he fulfilling that contract with Fort Cade without depleting his own stock? And why was it, for that matter, that half the scoundrels who swung at the end of Old Boy ropes had either worked for Weyburn's spread at one time or another, or were tied in with others who had? And another thing: Wasn't it odd that Till Cooke was murdered just when he was grinding Weyburn's nerves the hardest? What kind of man was the good sheriff anyway? Was he a murderer?

For David Weyburn, the days of Old Boy vengeance were also the days of personal decline. Bit by bit the public favor he bought with free drinks, big smiles, and friendly jokes began to fade. The same public to whom he had fed rumors of scandal involving Till Cooke and Claire O'Keefe quickly forgot those stories in the shadows of the far more intriguing speculations about Weyburn himself. Suspicions against him rose as respect for him declined—and then word got out somehow that District Attorney McBrearty was building a file on the sheriff, and talk grew all the hotter.

Weyburn became increasingly consumed by his difficulties, and it showed in his face. People speculated that he was ill, and in fact he had begun missing many days of work. He let deputies do his job for him while he remained closed up in his big stone house, mulling over his problems, thinking of resignation, then giving up that idea when he realized that sacrificing his office would make him lose almost all control of the stock theft network he operated from behind that sheriff's desk.

Locked away in his own private castle, Weyburn found little peace. As Magart's pregnancy advanced, she grew weak and ill, her joints swelling and her color draining away. Weyburn was reminded of the dearly beloved wife he had lost to childbirth some years before, and began to fear fate was about to hand him the same tragedy again. He spent much time beside Magart's bed, staring at her swollen belly, drinking, and saying things that frightened and repelled Maria Cruz. When Maria would repeat them to Eduardo in their room at night, he was just as horrified.

"He hates the child in her," Maria whispered to her husband. "He says he wishes it had never been conceived, and he hopes it dies before it kills his 'wife.' "

Eduardo would not comment when Maria repeated things like that. She could see the cowardice in him, and feared that in the end he would stand by and let even greater evils be done, rather than endanger himself. She began to despise him for it.

Weyburn didn't devote all his bedside rantings to Magart and her unborn child. He talked much about Till Cooke, cursing the former sheriff for dying in a manner that cast suspicion back on him. And he talked to Magart about her brother Jed—though Magart, in her brain-damaged state, had no more memory of him —and said he believed that Keller had taken up with the Old Boys in his fury over the death of Till Cooke. Even so—and this seemed odd to Maria Cruz—Weyburn didn't talk about Keller in the same tone as he talked of the late Cooke. He clearly held a certain odd respect for Keller, a deference to him that Maria could not understand.

Maria tucked away Jed Keller's name in her mind. When the time came for revealing hidden things, perhaps he could be the one she would turn to. After all, the Lady was his sister, and the child in her his blood kin.

When the autumn came, Cade's newspapers carried news of the wedding of Jed Keller and Claire O'Keefe. It was a sizable affair, and well-attended. Weyburn, to no one's surprise, was not invited to the wedding, but he made his presence known outside the church, watching the men who came out and noting down their names. Keller himself noticed the odd activity and wondered what Weyburn was up to. He would realize later that Weyburn operated under the assumption that he was a leader of the Old Boys, and that the men attending his wedding were likely to be Old Boys themselves.

And indeed many were. But Keller didn't worry

about it. In fact, he didn't fret nearly as much about Weyburn as he had before. He knew the man's prestige and power were declining—and that the nocturnal activities of the Old Boys seemed to lead ever closer to Weyburn's own door.

Cold nights descended on the Brazos country, and still the Old Boys rode, though the frequency of their excursions lessened as the number of thieves and rustlers plaguing the ranches was reduced.

Jed Keller was on the whole a happy man. Marriage to Claire brought him great joy and satisfaction, and for the first time in years he ceased to be haunted by dreams of that tragic shooting in the Missouri bank. Claire was a healing balm, soothing the most roughened and raw areas of his life.

But one thing undercut Keller's satisfaction: Cutter Wyeth remained at large. Everyone knew he was frequently in the county, for he was often seen, and he sometimes even sent out public taunts. The Old Boys, he declared, would never put a hand on him, and any who tried would draw back a bloody stump.

The Old Boys concentrated their efforts toward finding the outlaw. All they found was frustration. Wyeth had an uncanny ability to disappear like smoke, only to reappear somewhere else and issue another taunt and steal another horse. Keller began to despair of ever bringing Wyeth to justice.

One night Charlie Lilly came galloping up to the ranch house with exciting news for Keller. He had received information that Wyeth was holed up in a house at the remote area of Brock Spring, on the very western border of the county. Furthermore, he reportedly had some two dozen head of stolen cattle penned nearby, and was planning to steal more from Keller's herd—for Wyeth was said to believe that Keller now headed the Old Boys in Till Cooke's place, and was deliberately targeting his herd in retaliation.

"Where'd you hear this?" Keller asked Lilly.

"From Nancy Scarlet herself," Lilly answered. "She came here specifically to inform on Wyeth. She's mad at him again, and wants to be rid of him . . . with her own safety guaranteed, of course."

"I think we can accommodate her on both those scores," Keller said. "I think it would be advisable for us to pay a nighttime call on Brock Spring."

And so began the planning for what Keller and Lilly hoped would be the largest and most productive Old Boy excursion yet. This time, Keller was determined, Cutter Wyeth would not get away.

Then came an unexpected development. The day after Charlie Lilly brought his news, none other than David Weyburn himself rode onto the ranch, along with three deputies. When Keller came in answer, Weyburn dismounted, walked up to him, and informed him he was under arrest.

"Why am I being arrested?" Keller demanded.

Weyburn, his face so pallid and drawn that he looked like a different man than the Weyburn whom Keller had first met, looked him in the eye. "Nightriding and lynching, Mr. Keller. I'm taking you in for your part in the crimes of the so-called Old Boys."

"Do you have evidence to back your charges?" Keller said.

"That's a matter for later discussion," Weyburn replied. "You'll have an opportunity to defend yourself—which is more mercy than you have granted those who swing at the end of your ropes."

They unceremoniously hauled him off. He didn't even have time to say good-bye to Claire, nor to talk with Charlie Lilly, who watched the entire event with great concern.

Doyle Boston sidled up to Lilly as Keller was being taken down the road. "Do we ride, or does this stop us?"

Lilly seemed unsure. "Jed has wanted his personal

chance at Wyeth for a long time now. I despise taking it from him. But we may not find a better opportunity to get him. I think we ought to gather as many of the boys as we can and see what the feeling is."

Doyle Boston spat tobacco amber. "Fair enough—but I already know how I feel about it. I say let's ride, and let Cutter Wyeth stretch some hemp before sunrise. And if the others don't want to come, we can do it ourselves, just you and me. Cutter Wyeth ain't too much for two good men to handle, in my way of looking at it."

23

The events that followed the arrest of Jed Keller did so swiftly. Like dust devils that gust up separately, then join to form a large whirlwind, they combined to form an end that Keller himself could have never foreseen.

Keller paced in his cell, the lone prisoner in the jail. Claire had been here earlier, holding his hands through the bars and vehemently expressing her anger over his arrest. Keller had urged her to go home before darkness fell, and finally she had.

He went to the cell window. Somewhere out there, in that darkness to the west, the Old Boys were riding even now on a raid aimed at bringing down Cutter Wyeth once and for all. Keller wished himself among them. It was a shame to be stuck here while such an important event was taking place.

Restless, he shifted over to the cell door. "Deputy! Hey, out there! I'm thirsty! Can't a man get anything to drink in this lousy jail?"

The door leading to the front office opened and a man came through. Keller had expected one of the deputies. He had not expected David Weyburn.

"I'll be—so the devil himself oversees Hell tonight, eh?"

146

Weyburn smiled tightly. "This is far from Hell, and tonight I'm more your deliverer than your devil."

"I want a drink of water."

Weyburn reached up as if to tip a nonexistent hat. "At your service, Mr. Keller."

Keller was surprised when Weyburn actually did fetch him a cup of water. He couldn't imagine why the man would be kind to him.

"What was that talk about your being my deliverer, Weyburn?"

"Time will answer that question, Mr. Keller."

"Tell me: Why do you believe I lead the Old Boys?"

"Everything will come clear enough soon. As early as in the morning, I expect. Just be patient." The sheriff drew closer. "There's no cause for division between us, Mr. Keller. We have something in common, you and me."

"I've got nothing in common with you."

"Indeed you do . . . if only I were free to tell you about it."

Keller found Weyburn's cryptic manner irritating. He had heard enough obscurity; the time for free talking had come. "The truth is, Weyburn, I think I do know what you mean. You're talking about my sister."

Weyburn's reaction was more extreme than Keller would have anticipated. His eyes widened and he backed away. "What do you mean by that?" he said in a sharp whisper, even though there were no others present to hear.

"I know about the love affair between you and Magart. The one you carried on right under Folly Broadmore's nose just before Magart's death."

"Before Magart's death . . ." Keller wondered why Weyburn sounded almost relieved as he said those words.

"That's right. And since I'm speaking so freely, let me say something else that's been on my mind for a long time now. When I first came to Cade and found Magart was dead, I heard a rumor that Paco the Mex—remember him?—was hinting around that there was something out of the ordinary about the fire that killed the Broadmores. You know already that I tried to beat information out of Paco once when I was drunk. I didn't learn anything that time, but later on I had occasion to help out Paco, and he was ready to tell me. Only one thing stopped him, and that was the sight of Floyd Fells close by, within earshot. It nearly scared Paco to death. 'Weyburn's man,' he called Fells. That was the last day Paco was seen. You know what I think, Weyburn? I think Paco is dead, and that Floyd Fells killed him so he wouldn't have another chance to tell what he knew. And whatever it was that he did know, I think it comes around somehow right back to your doorstep."

Weyburn wore the darkest of expressions. "You're insane, Keller. You seem to be making some sort of major accusation against me."

"You catch on fast, Sheriff."

"Then what is it you're accusing me of? Spit it out!"

Now Keller could find little way to express himself. "The truth is, I don't know what I'm accusing you of," he said. "I've had a bad feeling about you ever since I first met you that day in the hallway at the Big Dakota. And it's not only because of your dealings with scum like Wyeth. It's because of Magart, and Paco, and whatever it was he would have told me if he had been given the chance."

"What could an old Mexican drunk have known that would be worth the telling?"

"You tell me, Sheriff. You sure enough seemed worried about what he might have told me the first time you and me ever talked."

Weyburn evidently was growing tired of this conversation. "I've got only one thing more to say to you, Keller, and that's that I've done you a favor you don't yet know about, though you will soon enough. And yes,

you're right—I did love your sister. That's the thing
we've got in common, and it's for her sake that I've
helped you today. Because she spoke so highly of you.
Because she loved you."

"I'm glad to know she did. That's information I can
truly thank you for. But tell me, Weyburn: How is it
that dragging me away from my own ranch and locking
me up in this jail equals out to 'helping' me? This is help
I can do without. You think Magart would have wanted
her brother treated this way?"

Weyburn smiled mysteriously. "Be patient, Jed Keller. Soon you'll understand." He turned on his heel and
headed out of the cell block. At the door he stopped and
looked back. "You think you're so clever, Keller. You
think you know so much. But you know nothing, nothing at all. There are things I could tell you that would
knock you onto your backside. If only you'd have the
sense to mind your own affairs."

For Keller, the moment was one of those when sud-
den insight rises with the clarity of a winter dawn. The
jumble of vague suspicions he had been carrying around
for months suddenly patterned themselves into a picture, or at least a potential picture. "Weyburn, did you
kill Folly Broadmore? Because he had beaten Magart?"

The sheriff held his silence, staring at Keller for several seconds with a peculiar expression. When he entered the front office, he slammed the cell-block door
behind him very hard.

It would have pleased Calvin McBrearty's healthy
sense of irony if he could have known of the conversation that was taking place between Keller and Weyburn
even as he was roused from sleep by a series of violent
knocks on his door. The big district attorney sat up,
rubbed his face and grumbled, "Hold your horses, whoever you are! I'm coming as fast as I can!"

He rose and put on his trousers, then stumbled
through his dark house to answer the knocking, which

continued despite his yells for patience. Just as he was reaching for the latch, he remembered something and paused long enough to slip off the mail-order, black-net mustache-shaping device he always wore to bed to make sure his most precious personal ornament didn't lose its beautiful form. He thrust the embarrassing item into his pocket as he opened the door.

"What the devil is it?" he blared as the door swung open. "Do you know what hour it is?"

The face on the other side was that of former Till Cooke deputy Haman Polk, who lately had been unhappily vegetating as a clerk in a local tack and feed store. Polk looked very upset.

"Mr. McBrearty, I'm awful sorry to bother you right now, but you need to come quick."

"What is it, Haman?"

"We've found something, Homer and me. A body. A dead body."

"A body? Where?"

"In Cade Creek, where it pools up deep behind the stone dam. We were out there camping and fishing and such. The corpse had rocks and things tied to it to keep it sunk, but the water had rotted away the ropes enough to let him come up . . . what's left of him. I'm sure it's a murdered man. Homer's still out there guarding him while I fetch you."

"Why did you come to me and not the sheriff?"

"Pshaw! It was Sheriff Weyburn who fired me and Homer, Mr. McBrearty. I won't go to him for nothing. Besides, I just plain-old don't trust him."

"You have keen insight, my friend. I don't trust him either." McBrearty stretched and yawned. "Well, so much for sleeping tonight. Come in and have a seat— we'll be off as soon as I get dressed."

Polk sat and fidgeted in his chair while he waited. McBrearty bumped around in his room, dressing too slowly to suit Polk. The district attorney called out through the half-open door, "Could you tell who the dead man was?"

"Not from the face," Polk said. "You know what water does to a body. But we think we know who it was anyway. He had only one leg, you see."

McBrearty all but lunged out of his room. "Paco the Mex?"

"Yes sir, I think it was. And from what little remains of him, I believe his throat was cut."

Keller sat up abruptly, making his cell bunk squeak. He had just experienced a second burst of insight. Weyburn's cryptic talk of "helping" him had suddenly taken on a grim kind of sense.

"No, no! Not that!" Keller leaped up and went to his cell window, looking out across the dark alley and toward the west. "God, please don't let it happen, not that. Not that."

He stared out into the dark, ridiculously trying to see what was impossible to see, for Brock Spring was many miles away. "Charlie," he whispered. "Charlie, what have you ridden into? God help us, what fools we've been!"

It was one of the darkest moments Jed Keller would know in his life.

Meanwhile, a couple of miles away, David Weyburn was also awake. Downstairs in his home office, he was dressed in a robe and was still very rumpled from sleep. Like Calvin McBrearty, he had been roused by a knock at his door.

His caller was Floyd Fells, and from Fells's expression, Weyburn knew his partner was not a happy man. Fells pushed his way in without waiting for an invitation.

"David, is it true?"

"Is what true?"

"You know what I mean! Is it true you arrested Jed Keller to keep him from going on the Old Boys raid?"

"I arrested him, yes."

"Damn! Do you know what you've done? You've brought the whole thing down around our heads!"

"What? You're talking loco, Floyd."

"No, David, no. It's you who's loco. Once Keller understands that he was arrested to protect him from that ambush, it's going to be obvious that you had knowledge of the ambush beforehand. In other words, you've as much as verified to the Old Boys that you and Wyeth work together, David. The Old Boys will be hanging you and me next!"

Weyburn glowered, spluttered, then said: "You worry too much, Fells. Nothing is going to happen." He didn't sound as confident as he intended, and in fact Fells saw that his words had shaken Weyburn. It astounded him to realize that such an obvious and dangerous flaw in planning had been both made and overlooked by the sheriff. Fells knew right then that Weyburn had already crossed a line. He had broken under the strains of the past weeks.

"It's over, David. There's no hope now."

"I did what I had to do! What else could I have done?"

"What else? You could have left well enough alone! You could have let Jed Keller ride into Brock Spring with the others. You could have let him die, and there would have been one less worry for us!"

"I couldn't let that happen—not to Keller."

"Why? Where does this great love for Jed Keller come from?" Fells waved his hand violently in a gesture of disgust. "Hell, I know where it comes from. It's because of *her*. That's it, ain't it!"

"He's her brother, Floyd! That means something, you know! I can't let the brother of my wife die like some dog out there under Wyeth's guns!"

"She ain't your wife, David, no matter how much

you call her that. She's nobody's wife now, just a widow. A widow who was beat into such a pulp by her late husband that she ain't hardly even a real woman anymore! But she is woman enough to bear a child, ain't she? And that child will be the death of us for sure, for there'll be no keeping that a secret, no matter what notions you have. God, I was a fool to have ever gone to work with you! I was a fool to have ever thought we could get away with all this! At one time I thought this might have worked—but now you've ruined it . . . all because of that mindless she-dog you've thrown away your good sense over!"

Weyburn drew back his fist and swung. Fells reached out and stopped the blow with a deft catch of Weyburn's forearm. The two men faced off silently, both drawing great heaving breaths. Fells said, "Don't you try to hit me again, David. Don't even think of it."

"If you ever talk to me like that, Floyd, I'll kill you. You don't talk about Magart that way and expect me to overlook it."

Fells slowly smiled, and the smile evolved into a cold laugh. "You know, David, we just handled it all wrong, didn't we! We made it too complicated. After you killed Folly Broadmore, we should have just taken Magart out, burned the house down around Broadmore's corpse, and had you marry Magart right out in the open sometime after. It would have been so simple, if you'd only have allowed it."

"It wouldn't have worked," Weyburn replied. "I'm still legally married to somebody else, and trying to marry Magart would have revealed that sooner or later. And even without that, there would have been no way. If I had married her, it would have generated talk. People would have figured out what had been going on between Magart and me; they might have even investigated Folly Broadmore's death a lot more closely and found the truth. And I sure as hell could have never been elected sheriff in the midst of all that suspicion. We did it the only way we could have."

Fells said, "That's clear thinking, David. I wish you could have been that clearheaded when you thought up the notion of saving Jed Keller from that ambush, for then you'd never have done such a fool thing. But it's too late now, ain't it! Before we know it, the Old Boys will be on us."

"Now it's you who've lost your clearheadedness. After tonight there won't be any Old Boys, remember? Except for Keller, they'll all be dead."

"If we're lucky."

"We will be. Trust me."

"I've already trusted you," Fells said. "And that's what's liable to get me hung."

He strode to the door and out into the night, leaving Weyburn staring after him through the doorway.

24

J ed Keller was released after breakfast the next morning. No explanations, no appearance by the sheriff.
Just a deputy who turned a key and told him he was
free to go, that his arrest had been an unfortunate mistake.

If not for the insight that had come in the middle of
the night, Keller would have been surprised. There was
no surprise now. This newest piece fit the puzzle perfectly, and only gave more credence to the terrible suspicion already in mind.

Keller had been hauled to jail on the back of a
wagon, and therefore had no mount upon which to ride
home. He headed for the South Brothers Livery to bor-
row or rent a horse, but he never made it that far. Along
the way he was hailed by Calvin McBrearty. Veering
across the street to meet McBrearty on the boardwalk,
Keller was surprised when the district attorney yanked
him into the closest alleyway, as if to avoid their being
seen together.

"McBrearty, I'm glad to see you. Let me tell you
what happened to me."

"No time, Keller. Listen to me: Paco the Mex has
been found."

"Alive?"

"Anything but. He was murdered, and his body was sunk in the pool behind the Cade Creek stone dam."

"Murdered! Then I'll bet the farm it was Floyd Fells who did it."

"I agree; the problem is, we have no clear proof."

"I'll be glad to testify as to Paco's fear of Fells."

"Thank you, but you are not the most credible witness where Paco is concerned, given the row you had with him."

"So what can be done?"

"What I want to do for now is nothing, at least nothing public. I don't want it known that Paco has been found, not until I can gather more concrete evidence. The Polk brothers found him; they can be trusted to keep quiet. The county coroner—who quite conveniently is married to my sister—has put the body on ice above his apothecary. He'll be conducting a quiet autopsy today or tomorrow. Thank our lucky stars that Paco had no immediate kin here who would require notification; otherwise we couldn't do this."

"What are you going to be looking for in the meantime?"

"Anything I can find, my friend. Any evidence at all that would more firmly establish Fells as Paco's murderer. But I won't be able to wait long. You can only sit on a murder so long, you know."

Keller said, "I'll help you any way I can. Now let me ask you something that isn't as unrelated as it might sound. Have you heard anything this morning about gun battle around, say, Brock Spring last night?"

McBrearty looked puzzled. "No. Should I have?"

"I hope not. Let's just say I have reason to suspect such a thing."

"You've both confused and intrigued me, Jed."

"I'm a mite confused myself. I was just turned out

of Weyburn's jail, hardly minutes before you yelled for me."

"You were jailed? For what?"

"For allegedly leading the Old Boys. That was the charge. As of this morning it must have been dropped, because they turned me out and said it had all been a mistake."

"But why—what—"

"Let me confuse you even more. According to Weyburn himself, I was arrested for my own protection."

"Protection from what?"

"From death at the hands of Cutter Wyeth—or that is my suspicion. I have reason to believe that the Old Boys rode last night. I have reason to believe they were lured to Brock Spring on hopes of finding Cutter Wyeth there. I believe it was all bait for an ambush."

"Jed, are you in fact leading the Old Boys?"

"If I wasn't, I'd be truthful and deny it. If I was, I'd be untruthful and still deny it. Suffice it to say that Weyburn believes I'm an Old Boy, and it was because of that he locked me up. So I wouldn't get killed."

"Why, in the name of heaven, would he want to protect you if he believes you are an Old Boy?"

"For the sake of my late sister, that's why. He was in love with her. He carried on an affair with her right under Folly Broadmore's nose. I even suspect he may have murdered Folly because he beat my sister so badly. Maybe he had beaten her badly enough to kill her, and so Weyburn killed him and set the fire to cover what he had done. Maybe Paco knew about that some way or another. I don't know—it's all guesswork. But whatever the case, Weyburn sure didn't want me roaming free last night."

"So the question is: Was there an ambush at Brock Spring last night?" McBrearty said. "If there was, then David Weyburn has made a fatal mistake. He's proven that he knew in advance that such a thing was planned, and that links him firmly with Cutter Wyeth."

"That's one piece of evidence I hope we don't find," Keller said. "Because if there was an ambush last night, you can bet the aim was to kill as many Old Boys as possible. And I hope to God that didn't happen. There's a lot of good—" And he cut off. He had been ready to say there were a lot of good men among the Old Boys, but at the last second had remembered that vigilantism was not legal, and this *was* the district attorney he was talking to.

McBrearty, keen-minded as he was, easily figured out what Keller had been about to say. He grinned. "Don't worry, my friend. At the moment I have more important fish to fry than trying to ascertain who makes up the Old Boys. In fact, I suspect that I'm so distracted right now by other matters that I might not recognize evidence of any individual's Old Boy participation if it were to stare me right in the face. Do you understand me?"

Keller grinned now. "I do. Now come on, Mc-Brearty. Let's head out to my spread and see if we can pick up any information about what might have happened at Brock Spring last night."

"We can take my buggy, if you'd like."

"Very good. Very good."

Taking back alleys to avoid public notice, they went around to McBrearty's private stable to fetch the rig. Within a few minutes they were rolling out of Cade toward Keller's ranch.

Within a mile of the ranch, they were met by Claire, who was riding at a fast clip back toward town. Keller was surprised not only by the meeting itself, but also by Claire's unkempt condition. She rode astride a man's saddle, wearing a pair of his trousers and an old shirt, her hair tucked up under a man's hat. Keller could think of only one reason Claire would go out publicly in that state: that she was in too great a hurry to do otherwise.

"Oh, no," he said to McBrearty as Claire drew near. "It must have happened. Just like I feared."

Claire, of course, was just as surprised to see Keller as he was to see her. She rode up and halted as McBrearty pulled the buggy to a stop.

"Jed, how did you get out?"

"I was turned loose, flat-out. Claire, this is Calvin McBrearty, district attorney."

"District attorney . . ."

"Don't worry. It's all right, and you can speak freely. Claire, was there trouble at Brock Spring last night?"

"Yes . . . but how did you know? That was what I was coming to town to tell you."

"Never mind. Was it an ambush?"

"Yes. Jed . . . Doyle Boston is dead."

Keller lowered his head. "I had hoped they got away clear."

"They didn't. And Charlie Lilly is hardly alive himself."

"What about others?"

"There were no others. When you were arrested, Charlie and Doyle were determined that . . . Jed, is it really all right to talk about this in front of the district attorney?"

"Ma'am, I seem to have gone deaf as a post," McBrearty said.

"Go on, Claire. He's with us on this."

"Charlie and Doyle wanted to go on after Wyeth just like they had planned. But when the others found out you had been arrested, they got wary and backed out. Charlie and Doyle went on alone."

"Alone? What a fool thing—"

"That's what I told them. They wouldn't listen. They went on and rode right into an ambush. Doyle fell dead at the first volley. Charlie managed to ride away— but he was shot up, bad. I don't think he would have gotten out alive at all except that Wyeth and his men were looking for a bigger group, and that distracted them from finishing Charlie off as quickly. He's back at the ranch right now, Jed, and I've already sent to town for the doctor. I don't know that he'll live."

"This clearly establishes that Weyburn and Wyeth are in league with one another," McBrearty said. "Not that I've been listening in."

"Jed, when I think how close you came to riding into that ambush . . ."

"You can thank David Weyburn for my safety," Keller said. "I was arrested to spare me from being with the Old Boys last night. He knew the ambush was coming, and he spared me, because he had loved Magart and I was her brother. Now let's get on to the ranch. I want to see Charlie Lilly."

The doctor arrived only minutes after they got back to the ranch. Keller was denied the opportunity to talk much to his injured friend. Not that Lilly was in shape to talk anyway; he had been shot three times, and was now hardly conscious and showed signs of losing his rationality.

It deeply depressed Keller to see the condition his friend was in. He sat brooding. McBrearty came to him, tugging his mustache and looking concerned.

"Change of plans. I'd best get Fells into custody soon, given what's happened," he said. "Fells is smart enough to figure out that Weyburn has tipped his hand by arresting you. He'll take out for parts unknown as soon as he sees things beginning to unravel."

"Who will you send to arrest him, with the sheriff being who he is?"

"If necessary, I'll get help from Fort Cade. I'm hoping, however, that some assistance will arrive today from the Texas Rangers. I wired for one or two men to come, if possible, to help me investigate Weyburn. They wired back that at least one would arrive today. If so, we'll go after Fells."

"What about Weyburn? Now that we can show he and Wyeth were in coordination on that ambush, you've got the nail you needed to hang him on."

"Yes . . . but only at the price of revealing your participation—not to mention that of Charlie Lilly and Doyle Boston—in the Old Boys. There may be legal repercussions coming from that that I'll be unable to control."

"In other words, I'll have to confess to being a vigilante, and take the potential consequences, if we're to bring down Weyburn."

"Exactly."

Keller drew in a long, deep breath. "All right. If that's what it takes, so be it."

"Not so fast, my friend. Give me time on this, and maybe there'll be evidence found that isn't so costly. For example, Mr. Fells himself might be persuaded to turn evidence against Weyburn in return for some sort of leniency. It's worth a try, at least—so don't go making any confessions just yet. Good day, my friends. And take good care of Mr. Lilly."

Keller and Claire sat up most of the night with Lilly, waiting for him to die. Fever rose in him and he went out of his head; throughout the night he spouted twisted and garbled poetry, yelled at sights no one else could see, and groped the air above him with his right arm, the left one being injured and immobile. When morning came he was still alive. Keller stayed with him all day, dozing in his chair, and when night came, Lilly was yet living.

Keller began to hope that Lilly would pull through. That became the only important thing to him. David Weyburn, Cutter Wyeth, the murder of Paco the Mex . . . none of it seemed to matter now. All Jed Keller cared about was seeing Charlie Lilly come through alive.

25

Floyd Fells tilted up the bottle and took another swallow of rye. It was four in the morning, and since his confrontation with Weyburn the previous night, he had been up drinking and worrying, hidden away in his little hut near the bunkhouse.

He knew it was time to leave, yet he was afraid to make the break. The idea of abandoning Weyburn filled him with fear. It would represent the final break between the two men, and while it might save him from being dragged down with Weyburn, it also would end any protection the sheriff had to offer. If he fled, Weyburn would certainly use him as a scapegoat, should one become necessary.

It was a matter of weighing risks, and Fells couldn't make up his mind. He drank again, then put the bottle aside. He was close to being drunk already, and if he fled, he needed to have his wits about him.

The longer he thought about it, the more appealing flight became. Especially now that he knew the outcome of the ambush at Brock Spring. Rather than destroy the Old Boys, as had been the hope, the ambush had succeeded in killing one, maybe two men—the only two who had snapped at the bait of Cutter Wyeth. The ambush had been a failure—and no doubt the reason was that Jed Keller's arrest had spooked the majority of the Old Boys off the chase. Thanks to Weyburn, the Old Boys were still around, and now had every reason to focus their attention on Weyburn . . . and on he himself, by extension.

The risk of remaining in Cade was simply too great. Fells made up his mind right then. He would go. Let Weyburn deal with the outcome of his own foolishness alone. Even if what Weyburn had already done didn't bring him down, the birth of Magart Broadmore's child would. And that was due to occur at any time.

"Yes, sir," Fells said to himself. "Time to get while the getting's good."

His spirits brightened now that his mind was made up. He knew he had made the right choice. *I was a fool to stay this long. I'll ride to Arkansas, Kansas, Missouri, even Mexico—anywhere but Texas. I can change my name, line myself up a job, and be safe. They'll never find me once I'm out of Texas.*

He took two horses, one belonging to him and the other to Weyburn. Fells owned few personal possessions, and what he couldn't pack with him on horseback he simply left. None of those things mattered now. What mattered was freedom.

He rode through the predawn darkness over toward the main road. When he reached it, the sun was sending the first splinters of light across the horizon. When Weyburn's big house came into view, Fells paused only a moment.

"Good-bye, David Weyburn," he said aloud. "When you hang, you'll hang without Floyd Fells beside you."

He spurred his horse and headed down the road, wanting to put as much distance as possible behind him before full daylight.

*   *   *

Fells was unaware of the three men who watched him traveling over the rolling terrain. One of the three was Calvin McBrearty, who studied Fells through a pair of binoculars borrowed from one of the two men beside him. Both of McBrearty's companions wore the badge of the Texas Rangers. The men had arrived late the prior day, and the first order of business today was the arrest of Floyd Fells for the murder of the Mexican named Paco.

"That's Fells, all right," McBrearty said, handing back the binoculars. "If we'd have waited another hour, we'd have lost our chance at him."

"Reckon he was tipped off about the Mexican's corpse being found?" one of the Rangers asked.

"I doubt it," replied McBrearty. "I'd say the reason that bird is flying its coop is simple common sense. He knows that Weyburn made a bad mistake when he arrested Jed Keller."

"We'll find out soon enough, I reckon." The Rangers began riding forward.

"Gentlemen—when you take him in, don't tell him about the murder suspicion right away. If need be, let him believe his arrest relates to stock theft. I'm interested in hearing what he'll have to say on his own steam."

"Whatever suits you," one of them said. They put spurs to flanks and headed out after Floyd Fells. McBrearty watched them a little while, then rode back toward Cade to await their return.

Fells felt the beginning of panic when he realized there was someone behind him on the road. Two men, he believed, though he had caught only a distant and fleeting view and could not be sure. Why were they following him—or were they merely other travelers who happened to be on the same road?

He couldn't bet on the latter. He would have to

assume he was being followed until given proof to the contrary.

The land made a steady upturn for the next quarter mile. Fells pushed his mount harder until he topped the rise, then descended just as quickly. Ahead and to the right was a thick grove of oaks growing along a stream. He left the trail, entered the trees, dismounted and tethered the horses. Drawing his rifle from its saddle boot, he crept to the edge of the tree line and took shelter behind a stump.

From here he had a good view of the road, while remaining out of sight himself. Leveling his rifle, he watched the spot where the two riders would appear.

Within a few moments a rider came across—only one. Fells was confused. What had happened to the second man? He began looking furtively around, thinking some sort of trick was afoot. The lone rider continued on, his horse moving at a steady but unhurried pace. The rider whistled to himself and didn't appear to be looking for anyone or anything in particular. By all appearances, he was merely a traveler on his way to wherever he was going. He rode on over the next low hill and was gone.

Fells frowned. Might he have been mistaken about there being two riders? Surely he had been. He stood and leaned against a tree trunk, giving himself comforting mental counsel. Of course there had been only one rider, and he wasn't in pursuit of anyone.

Fells returned to his horse and booted the rifle. He felt much better now. Downright secure, in fact. He had made it out. He would be long gone before Weyburn or anybody else even noticed.

He waited to give the rider ahead a longer lead, then headed out onto the road again. He traveled more slowly than before. The ups and downs of the road increased, so that Fells had less and less range of view both in front and behind. He paid no attention to this; he was relaxed now, halfway dozing in the saddle.

Something jerked him out of his daze. He stopped, confused and concerned, realizing that he had been completely asleep for a few moments. He straightened and looked all around him.

And behind him. His heart surged. Another rider was there. Traveling alone, just like the first. Fells watched him coming over the rise. Fells turned and began riding forward more quickly, wary of this newcomer. *Calm down,* he told himself. *This is just another traveler, like the first one. Mind your own business, and he'll mind his.*

Then he came across the next rise. In the middle of the road ahead sat the first rider, his horse crossways in the road and his rifle out and resting butt down against his thigh. Fells stopped, gaping. The man pulled back his coat, and the sun caught the glint of a badge.

Fells pivoted his horse to run, and saw the rider behind him coming up. His rifle was out as well, and he too wore a badge. Fells looked around, and crazily pictured himself bolting across the countryside, all pursuers left behind as he rode to freedom. Then reality set in. He couldn't run. He knew those badges. These were Texas Rangers, men trained in pursuit, men who would hound him until his horse fell from under him, then hound him some more until he had run himself into the ground.

They advanced from both sides. "Floyd Fells?"

"Yes. I'm Fells."

"Mr. Fells, my name is Bill Childress, and yonder is Landal McTavish. We're officers of the Texas Rangers, and we're authorized by the district attorney of this county to bring you in for questioning."

Fells bowed his head, and to his own surprise began to cry. "I'm sorry," he said, swiping at his tears. "It's just that I thought I had made it out safe. I really thought I had. I reckon this is about the cattle and such. At least you aren't the Old Boys, huh?"

"No, we're not. We'll take those weapons, Mr.

Fells," McTavish said. "You won't be needing them at the moment."

Fells cried all the way back to Cade, shaming himself, yet unable to stop. "I'm sorry," he said again and again. "I'm mighty embarrassed."

As for the Rangers, they had nothing to say at all.

26

Only with great effort did David Weyburn force himself out of bed with the sun. It took an even more excruciating push to get through his breakfast and onto his horse for the ride into town.

Weyburn was a frightened man. Despite his deliberate bravado in assuring Fells that his worries were groundless, Weyburn knew now that he had made a major mistake. He felt like a fool. How could he have failed to understand what he was doing?

He felt weary, confused, and had a sense of mounting desperation so intense that it caused a buzzing in his ears. He feared that his days as sheriff were numbered, and that probably it had been a mistake to take this job in the first place. He had believed that as sheriff he could control with impunity the entire network of stock thieves on the Brazos. It hadn't worked that way, thanks to the Old Boys, and thanks to his own obsessed devotion to Magart.

Weyburn looked around as he rode, and longed to ride out of this county and not look back. But he couldn't. There was Magart to think of, and the child she was about to give birth to. Maria Cruz believed the baby would be born this very week, possibly in the next day or so. Weyburn had left word with his servants to come fetch him as soon as the first signs of labor came on.

Lord, but I'm tired this morning, Weyburn thought. He hadn't slept much the night before. Too much on his mind. And when he had slept, he dreamed about the Tonkawa woman Floyd Fells had killed, and about Paco the Mex. He felt guilty for their deaths, even though it hadn't been his hand that killed them. They had both died because of him, and that didn't sit easily on his mind. Perhaps Floyd Fells had no conscience, but David Weyburn did. More of a conscience than he had realized.

Weyburn had broken out in a sweat by the time he reached his office, and as he dismounted he felt dizzy. Might he be getting sick? He was actually happy to consider that possibility, for an oncoming illness would explain the nightmares, the sense of coming doom, the buzzing in his ears.

He stabled his horse in the shed behind the jail and went inside. The night deputy at the desk was snoring, and looked embarrassed when he woke up and saw Weyburn looking at him. He stood.

"Morning, Sheriff."

"Morning."

The deputy frowned. "Are you feeling all right, Sheriff Weyburn? You look a little green this morning."

"I think maybe I'm coming down with something. But I'll be fine. Go on home, and we'll see you back tonight."

Weyburn felt relieved when the deputy was gone. An examination of the cell block revealed that the jail had no prisoners. Even better. Weyburn poured himself a cup of coffee, spiked it with whiskey from a pocket flask, added a dollop of molasses from the shelf above the stove and a chunk of hard candy from a sack in his desk. Looking for further signs of illness, he had convinced himself his throat felt raw. This concoction should help.

When he had finished drinking, he rose, went to the window, and surveyed the busy main street of Cade. He turned his face in the direction of his own house and wondered how Magart was faring. Her labor could be starting even now. He remembered the death of his first wife in childbirth, and wished he could call in a doctor to help Magart through her own delivery. That was out of the question, of course. Magart was supposedly dead and buried. What help she received in labor would have to come from Maria Cruz.

Weyburn went back to his desk, rubbing the back of his neck and letting his thoughts proceed a step further. He had managed to hide Magart well enough, but what would he do with the baby? Fells was right; there would be no hiding an infant.

It's not going to work. There's no way it can work. I'll have to get rid of the baby. Maybe Eduardo can haul it off and drop it at the door of some church or orphanage.

The idea made him feel even more conscience-stricken. That was Magart's child he was thinking about —Magart's, and his own. Perhaps the thing to do would be to leave, as soon as the baby was old enough . . .

. . . if the Old Boys allow me that much time. After what happened at Brock Spring, they'll be out for my blood. God above, what's going to happen here? Magart, how are we going to get ourselves out of this?

David Weyburn pulled the flask from his pocket, turned it up, and took a long, shaky swallow.

"I must go get him at once!" Eduardo Cruz held his wife by the shoulders and virtually spat the words into her face. "He has given us clear instruction, and if we disobey, he will hold us to account!"

"And you fear him, don't you, my husband? You are more afraid of the wrath of David Weyburn than of the wrath of the God who will smite both him and us if we continue to do wrong!"

"And what would you have us do, woman? Deliver her child and steal it away?"

"Yes, that is exactly what I would have us do. This child is an innocent one, Eduardo. Nothing good can come to it, being born into this household! It would be sent away . . . maybe killed. When the child comes, the days of Señor Weyburn's secrets will be short. The baby would be discovered in time, and the truth would come out, all of it. There is danger for this child here . . . we cannot let harm come to a baby, my husband! We cannot!"

Eduardo cursed and pushed her away. Pacing back and forth, he sought escape from the predicament and could not find it. He went to the bedside of Magart Broadmore and looked down into her ashen face. His fear increased, for even he, who knew nothing of childbirth, could see that Magart's labor was not proceeding correctly. What if she should die in childbirth, like David Weyburn's first wife had? Weyburn would blame him for that—especially if they failed to notify him promptly, as they had been directed.

"Maria, there is no other way—I must go to Señor Weyburn. There is nothing else to do."

"Yes, there is," Maria said. "We can bring the child into the world and take it away to safety, out of his reach. We can for once in our lives do what is right!"

"Take it away? How would we care for a newborn child, wife? There is no milk in your old breasts!" He paused, then tried a shift of tack. "And Señor Weyburn would certainly pursue us, and when he found us, he would be angry, and then the child truly would be in danger. For the sake of the child, we must go to Señor Weyburn now."

"For the sake of the child, you say? Bah!" Maria spat at her husband's face. "It is only because of your cowardice, Eduardo. The man I have married is a coward! Very well, then! Go to Señor Weyburn, if you must! But may the blood of this child be on your hands!"

Eduardo's face was red with fury. He pivoted and stalked out of the room. Maria listened as he stomped down the stairs and out the door. At the window she watched him cross to the stable and saddle a horse. A few minutes later he was galloping off toward Cade.

Now it was her turn to be fearful. Maria closed her eyes and prayed fervently. *God, bring the child quickly, before Weyburn returns. Give me time to take it away to a safe place . . . but where?*

She lifted her head. Yes! Now she knew where she could take the child—if only it would be born quickly enough. Repeating the prayer in her mind, she went to Magart's bedside.

Magart opened her eyes, and from her throat boiled up a yell of pain. This was a fast and painful labor, and Magart's suffering brought tears to Maria's eyes. She put her hand on Magart's brow.

"Be strong, Lady," she said. "You must push the child from your body. Be strong. I am with you."

It was a mustache-stroking moment for Calvin McBrearty, for he was satisfied. Before him sat Floyd Fells, a very scared man. *But not nearly so scared,* McBrearty thought privately, *as he will be when I show him the iced-down body at the coroner's. That will probably be enough to make him start crying again.*

"Mr. Fells, may I ask you where you were going this morning?" McBrearty asked, pulling a cigar from his pocket.

"Riding. That's all. Just riding away."

"For good?"

"Reckon so."

"You were leaving Mr. Weyburn's employment, then?"

"Yeah, yeah I was."

"Why?"

Fells shrugged. "Just wanted to. Tired of working there, you know."

"Tell me, Mr. Fells: How have you been fulfilling Mr. Weyburn's contract with Fort Cade? What is it . . . three beeves a day?"

"That's easy enough. I cut out three good beeves from the herd, slaughter and skin the hides off them, and haul them to the fort."

"What do you do with the hides?"

Fells paled a little. "Just get rid of them, you know."

"Where?"

His Adam's apple bobbed toward his chin and down again. "Throw them in the water."

"Mr. Fells, I think you know what I'm trying to get at. What water?"

"There's a pool by the slaughter pen. A stream we diverted and dammed. I throw them in there."

"I see. Thank you, Mr. Fells. Let me tell you something. I believe that when we go fish some of those hides out of that water, we'll find lots of brands on them other than Weyburn's. In fact, I suspect we won't find any Weyburn cattle at all. What do you think, Mr. Fells?"

No answer.

"The water may yield up some interesting evidence for us. It has a way of doing that, you know. As a matter of fact, let's walk down a couple of buildings here and let me show you something else the water has revealed for us. I think you might find it of personal interest."

Fells looked for all the world like a man walking to the gallows as they trudged behind the building row to the local apothecary. The druggist had some medical training and doubled as county coroner, and whenever he had to keep a body in storage, he iced it down in a sealed room on the second floor of the building, a big empty room like a warehouse.

The coroner was a tall and rather coarse man, and

the more dramatic McBrearty was somewhat disappointed by the slow and mundane way his brother-in-law opened the ice chest and lifted the top block to reveal Paco the Mex's much-decayed face. The disappointment was short-lived. What the coroner's performance had lacked in dramatic flair, Fells more than made up for by his reaction. He looked as if Hell itself had opened before him.

"That's Paco the Mex in there," McBrearty said. "I'm willing to bet you can tell us how he managed to get his throat so terribly sliced."

Fells darted out of the little room so quickly that not even the Rangers—who were distracted by the hideous corpse—could stop him. "No!" Fells screamed. "I didn't kill him! I didn't do it!"

He lunged for the stairs and made the top of them before the stunned lawmen could even get out of the ice room. McBrearty came out just in time to see Fells slip and tumble down the stairs. He made a horrible racket that ended with a thump like an unripe melon dropped on the bottom of an overturned barrel.

McBrearty pounded over to the stairs. Fells lay at the bottom, blood pulsing out of his nose and his eyes staring upward. In the process of falling, he had managed to strike his head very hard against the corner of one of the stairs. The pulsing of the blood stopped as McBrearty came to the bottom of the stairs.

"I'm confounded!" he said. "He's dead!"

Texas Ranger Bill Childress said, "Well, in all my days I ain't never seen one go out like that! No sir."

The coroner reached the bottom of the stairs last of all. He examined Fells's corpse briefly and said, "Well, if you carry him out through the apothecary, please try not to drip any blood on the floor."

When they hauled the body of Floyd Fells out of the apothecary and laid it out on a board, it drew a crowd very quickly. Down the street, David Weyburn had just stepped out of his office. Noting the tumult, he strode up the boardwalk.

The people murmured as he drew near, for they knew Fells worked for Weyburn. The crowd parted and let Weyburn through. He stared wordlessly at the body, then turned away. At that moment he looked almost as corpselike as Fells himself.

Eduardo Cruz galloped around the corner on the opposite end of the street. His goal was the sheriff's office, but he also was attracted by the crowd. He was about to descend from his horse and go over to see what was getting so much attention, when a momentary shift of the crowd allowed him to see the corpse.

A great fear gripped Eduardo. Fells . . . dead? He looked up and saw Weyburn striding away, his back toward him, his stride stiff, and the crowd looking from Fells to Weyburn and back again, and all Eduardo could think was: *Señor Weyburn has killed him. Señor Weyburn has become loco and killed Floyd Fells!*

The notion made little sense, but Eduardo was already agitated beyond clear thought. And Weyburn indeed had been acting lately like a man about to go over the edge of sanity.

Panic set in, and Eduardo wheeled his horse, riding away as fast as he could, out of Cade and onto the plains beyond, his mission of announcing Magart's labor forgotten.

27

McBrearty walked into the sheriff's office without knocking. A trace of Floyd Fells's blood had remained unnoticed on his fingers, and it wiped off on the knob as he turned it. McBrearty shuddered. He was a tough man, but blood always bothered him.

Weyburn was sitting at his desk. He looked like his spirit had been beaten out of him. His pallor was so deathly that McBrearty had to struggle not to gape at the man.

"Weyburn, you aren't looking so good these days," McBrearty said.

"It's not been an easy time for me. Vigilantes, rumors and accusations in the streets . . . and now it appears my foreman is dead."

"Yes. It was accidental." McBrearty told the story, starting with Fells's arrest. When he mentioned the part about the body of Paco the Mex, Weyburn gave a little spasm, like he had been kicked.

"So Paco the Mex was murdered?" Weyburn asked.

"Yes . . . but you knew that already."

Weyburn held his silence. No denials, no confirmations. Just that sad, blank stare. McBrearty had seen that expression before, on the faces of murder defendants when the evidence was strong against them and conviction inevitable. It was the expression of men looking over the nearing horizon and seeing death grinning and waiting for them to arrive.

"Mr. McBrearty, is it true you've been investigating me?"

"Yes, sir. I started it at the request of Till Cooke while he was still in office. What began out of his interest has continued out of my own. Mr. Weyburn, I believe that you have been, and are continuing, an involvement in stock theft. I believe that you, mostly through Mr. Fells, have worked in cooperation with Cutter Wyeth. I believe you had advance knowledge of the planned massacre of the vigilantes at Brock Spring. Is my line of thinking generally correct?"

Weyburn said, "You know I can't answer a question like that, Mr. McBrearty."

Interesting, McBrearty thought, *that he doesn't simply deny it. What has happened to this man?* He recalled what he had learned of the madness of Weyburn's grandfather, and wondered if Weyburn was moving toward a similar breakdown.

"There's more, Mr. Weyburn, though it is much less precise. You may be aware that Mr. Jed Keller has some vague suspicions that you know something about the death of his sister, something that Paco the Mex was killed to cover up. We believe it was Mr. Fells who killed him, though obviously that matter won't come to trial, given what has just happened. Might there be any substance to these suspicions?"

Weyburn gave no indication he had even been listening.

"Mr. Weyburn," McBrearty said gently, "I think you should consider turning in your badge. Difficult times are ahead for you, and for the sake of the operation of this county office, I think your resignation would be a helpful and appropriate gesture. You needn't admit guilt to any crime by so doing. It would merely be, as I said, a gesture showing your concern that this office's reputation not be sullied."

Weyburn reached under his vest, unpinned his badge, and laid it on his desk. "I was tired of it anyway," he said. "It seems I'm tired all the time now, Mr. McBrearty."

"Yes." McBrearty reached over and took the badge. "Perhaps a letter to the county court would be in order."

"Yes. I'll do that. I will." Weyburn's weary eyes lifted to McBrearty's face. "Am I under arrest?"

"No. I do anticipate the likelihood of an indictment soon, with later ones probable. I see no reason not to tell you. You are an intelligent enough man; you would have figured it out for yourself soon enough."

"Yes."

"I advise you, sir, don't try to flee the area. You know you would soon be found, and even if not, what kind of life would it be, looking over your shoulder the rest of your days?"

Weyburn nodded. He stood, still wearing that same sad and listless expression. Oddly, he thrust out his hand to McBrearty. Surprised, the district attorney shook it. It was like grasping a wet roll of newspaper.

"You are a credit to your position, Mr. McBrearty," Weyburn said. "Our county is well-served by its prosecutor."

Weyburn put on his hat and coat and walked out, leaving McBrearty thinking that in all his career in law, this conversation was the strangest he had ever held with any man, be he criminal, victim, judge, or juror.

David Weyburn spent the rest of the day riding alone on the plains around Cade. No longer did he feel that his world was about to crash around him. The crash had already come. Floyd Fells was dead, the district attorney apparently had a strong case building against him, and there was no way out now by denials and alibis.

Odd though it was, David Weyburn was relieved. He had tried to shoulder too big a burden, and now it had fallen back on him. He couldn't hope to lift it off now, even though it certainly would crush him. There was no more need for struggle, and the end of struggle was welcome.

As the day waned, Weyburn turned his mount toward his ranch. The sight of his big house brought a smile. Inside was Magart, the one being in the world he loved more than himself. Once they came after him, even Magart would be lost to him, and he knew it. Tonight he wouldn't let it matter. He would be with her, a man and his beloved, for whatever time they were given.

He wondered when the baby would come. It brought him pause, and he recalled the thought he had played with that morning, that the child would have to be sent away to preserve his precious secrets. Well, it didn't matter now. Soon enough there would be no secrets. The truth was going to come out, and not a thing he could do would stop it now.

He halted. Why was the house so dark? Why did it seem so empty?

"*Magart* . . ."

He dismounted at the gate and ran toward the door. It was ajar; he pushed it open and went inside. Not a light burned inside.

Weyburn drew his pistol and edged farther in. "Hello?"

No response. "Maria? Eduardo? Where are you?"

Silence. Then a scuffling, a movement upstairs—in Magart's room.

"Magart? Magart, are you all right?"

He ran up the stairs, taking four at a bound. Turning down the hall, he stopped, overcome by the darkness of the enclosed space. Just as he was digging in his pocket for a match, a light flared in Magart's bedroom.

Weyburn heard the clink of a lamp chimney being set in place, and the light smoothed and regulated.

Weyburn drew in a breath, edged forward, and leaped into the doorway, pistol leveled before him.

Eduardo Cruz looked back at him. He was holding the lamp, standing by Magart's bed. Weyburn lowered the pistol. "Eduardo?" Then he looked at Magart.

That she was dead was obvious at first glance. Unbreathing, gray of pallor, her head turned to the side, she lay between sheets bloodied by birthing, and her belly, formerly large with child, was flat under the top sheet.

"Magart, oh God, Magart!" Weyburn dropped the pistol and went to the bedside, falling to his knees. "Magart, have I lost you too? Have I lost you too?"

"I am sorry, Señor Weyburn," Eduardo said. He was shaking, making the flame of the lamp quiver, the distorted shadows of broken men it cast onto the wall in shuddering motion. "I came to town today to tell you of her labor, but I saw the body of Mr. Fells and grew afraid. I hid on the plains all day, but when it was dark I came back to see what had happened. I didn't know she had died, Mr. Weyburn. I didn't know. I'm so sorry, so very sorry."

"Where is Maria?"

"I don't know, Mr. Weyburn. She is gone."

"The baby . . ."

"There is no baby here, sir. Maria must have taken it."

Weyburn stood. "Taken it? Where?"

"I don't know, sir. I truly don't."

Weyburn looked at his pistol where it lay on the floor. Eduardo saw it too, and gave a little gasp of realization. He moved as if to go toward it, then his cowardice asserted itself and he cringed back. Weyburn walked over and picked up the pistol. He lifted it and aimed it at Eduardo.

"Señor Weyburn, please . . ." Eduardo knelt, setting the lamp before him on the floor and putting clenched fists on each side of his head. His eyes looked up pleadingly at Weyburn.

"You should have found me, Eduardo. You should have told me what was happening."

"I was afraid, sir. I am sorry—please don't kill me!"

Weyburn held the pistol up a quarter minute more, then lowered it. His manner softened. "Go away, Eduardo. Take a horse and ride away from here. One more death will solve nothing. It's over. It's all over."

Eduardo, trembling and cringing like a kicked dog, edged for the door, then went out it on a run.

Weyburn stood, stoop-shouldered, pistol in hand, in the center of the room. On the bed lay the shell of what had once been Magart Keller Broadmore, now cold and silent, and outside there was no sound but the receding hoofbeats of Eduardo Cruz's horse.

28

Magart Broadmore's baby boy wasn't born for almost three hours after Eduardo left to find David Weyburn. Maria could not guess what kept Eduardo and Weyburn from returning during that time—but whatever it was, it was a blessing. It allowed her time to get the child into the world and safely away from Weyburn's house.

She had cried when she realized Magart Broadmore had not survived the birthing. To see the life depart from one body even as it pushed a new life into the world seemed infinitely sorrowful, especially considering the sad condition in which Magart had lived during her last months. It made Maria despise David Weyburn. If not for the necessity to preserve his vile secrets, Magart Broadmore could have had the assistance of a doctor as she gave birth. She might have lived.

After the child was born, Maria was in a quandary. The baby was screaming for its mother's breast, but its mother could give it no sustenance now or ever. Maria cleaned the squalling newborn as best she could and wrapped it in a blanket, struggling against panic. "Don't cry, little one, I will take you to safety," she said. "I will find a breast to give you milk. I promise you. All will be well."

As she took the baby outside and over to the stable, she was grateful that Weyburn had built his house out of view of the working headquarters of the ranch. It gave her privacy to hitch a horse to a wagon without being observed or heard, for at the moment there were no living humans here except for herself and the crying baby. With nervous fingers she had finished the hitching —an unfamiliar job for her—and then climbed aboard, the enwrapped baby in her arms. She gave one last, tense look around to reassure herself that Eduardo and Weyburn were not coming into view, then drove off toward the ranch of Jed and Claire Keller.

Claire hadn't felt so sad since the day her uncle Till had died. She was alone in the ranch house. Jed was gone, along with a couple of the hands, taking Charlie Lilly into town to be put under the full-time supervision of the doctor. Despite his tenacious clinging to life, Lilly had taken a turn for the worse in the night, and it was evident, to Claire at least, that he was not going to survive.

Wiping her moist eyes on her cuff, she went to the window and looked across the ranch land. It was barren this time of year—as barren as she felt inside. It would be a sad thing to lose Charlie Lilly, a man ever bright and full of poetry. And all because the good men of the area had found themselves without any help in the official legal structure of the county. Even while reluctantly acknowledging the need for the Old Boys and their rough justice, Claire despised the fact they had existed— and especially that they had involved her husband so deeply. She had also come to despise David Weyburn, whose corruption and ineffectiveness as a law enforcement official were the ultimate reasons the Old Boys had been revived. If not for Weyburn, Till Cooke would probably still be alive, and Jed Keller wouldn't have violated his own pledge never to become a vigilante.

Claire's thoughts were interrupted by the sight of

an approaching wagon. At first she thought it was Keller and the hands returning from delivering Lilly to Cade and the doctor. Quickly she saw that it wasn't; this was a strange wagon, being driven by a woman—and clumsily driven at that. As it drew closer, Claire saw that the woman had a bundle in her arms, carefully held . . . like a baby.

It *was* a baby. Surprised, Claire threw her coat over her shoulders and left the house. The woman, who appeared to be Mexican, saw her, steered the wagon directly toward her, and came to a stop. The baby was squalling, but it was a weak and meager squall, like that of a newborn. Claire looked more closely, and was amazed to see that the baby appeared to be mere hours old at the most.

"My heavens, is that your child?" she asked, rushing forward with arms out. "Have you driven yourself here after giving birth?"

"No, señora, no . . . it is not my child. But please, we must find food for him."

"Yes, you are right. Come in, Miss, Missus . . ."

"I am Maria Cruz. Señora Keller, how will we feed him?"

After a few moments of thought, Claire said, "There's a camp of Indians west of the ranch, and one of the women has given birth. I'll send a man to tell her she can make good money as a wet nurse at the Keller place."

"Gracias, thank you so much," Maria said. "I can see you are a good woman, señora. And I have much to tell you and your husband."

"My husband is away at the moment."

"But I must see him. I have news for him, about his sister."

"About Magart Broadmore?"

"Si, señora. The child, you see, it is hers."

"But this is a newborn, and Magart Broadmore has been dead for almost a year."

"I will explain it all, señora, as soon as the child is fed."

The process of sending for and awaiting the Indian woman took a little more than an hour. During that time Claire was immensely curious, and also wondering if this Mexican lady was a madwoman. Might she have stolen this child from someone nearby? The baby's increasingly hoarse and weak crying made it impossible for Claire to question Maria Cruz very closely. Only when the somber-faced young Tonkawa arrived and put the hungry infant to her milk-swollen breast did the opportunity for explanation come.

"Tell me, now, Mrs. Cruz, how it is possible for a woman long dead to have given birth to a newborn baby."

"I see you do not believe me, señora. I don't blame you. What I have to tell will be difficult for you to believe. But you must believe it—and forgive me for my part in this terrible thing."

Then Maria Cruz began to talk, telling the story from the beginning, and when she was done, Claire Keller was a woman astonished. Maria's tale was as astounding as she had indicated it would be, but the more Claire thought about it, the more it fit the facts of the past year's experiences.

Jed Keller did not return home until late in the night, and from the expression on his face, Claire knew that Charlie Lilly had not lived. She met Keller outside, while the hands who had accompanied him saw to putting away the wagon.

"He went out easy, at least," Keller said. "At the end, for a couple of minutes, he was as lucid as he could be. That happens sometimes with folks who are dying. He gave me the name of his brother in Missouri and told me how to get hold of him. I've already had a wire sent. Charlie will be buried in the city cemetery." Keller paused, having heard something he couldn't identify. "What was that? It sounded like a baby."

"It is a baby."

"What? Here?"

"Yes. Come inside, Jed. There's a Mexican woman here, named Maria Cruz."

"Maria Cruz? Isn't that one of David Weyburn's house servants?"

"Yes. Jed, she has brought a baby here. A newborn. And she has a story to tell that you may find hard to bear. It has to do with your sister, and David Weyburn, and this new baby . . . but come in. I'll let her tell it."

Maria Cruz had calmed significantly since the morning, and spoke in a steady, even voice. Jed Keller sat holding the sleeping newborn as he listened in astonishment, trying to fathom what he already had been told: that the baby had been born that very morning to none other than his sister; that Magart had died only hours before, not months ago, as he had believed.

"What I tell you is what I know from my own experience, along with what has been told to me by my own husband. I will not pretend that I have no guilt; I ask only that you forgive me as best you can.

"I and my husband have worked for Señor Weyburn for several years. We knew well the kind of man he was, and had learned to turn our backs on it, God forgive us. We were with him when he came to the Brazos country and built his big house. We knew of his thieving and rustling, and that he dealt with bad men like Cutter Wyeth—but we said nothing, and did nothing. He was our employer, and we were faithful to him. Too faithful, I now know.

"Señor Weyburn fell in love with Magart Broadmore almost as soon as he first saw her. She was not a free woman, but a married one. And Señor Weyburn was not free either, though only those closest to him—my husband and I, and in time, Floyd Fells— knew he still had a wife who had refused to divorce him. But Señor Weyburn is not a man who can resist what he wants, and soon he and Magart Broadmore were involved in a love affair. At the beginning, Folly Broadmore knew nothing of what was going on, but in time he grew suspicious. He was a harsh man, Folly Broadmore, and cruel to his wife. As he grew more sure she was being untrue to him, his cruelty became worse. He began beating her—and that was what finally led to his end.

"Though no one now living knows exactly what happened, somehow Folly Broadmore found out it was David Weyburn who was seeing his wife. He grew terribly angry, and beat his poor wife until her head was almost crushed. It changed her, robbed her of her mind. She became simple, like a child, hardly knowing who she was, and remembering very little of her own life.

"When Señor Weyburn saw her in this way, he became furious. Floyd Fells was his foreman and partner by then, and they were together when Señor Weyburn went to make Folly Broadmore pay for what he had done. I don't know exactly how he killed him, but I think he stabbed him to death, right in Folly Broadmore's own house, and right before Magart's eyes. But she didn't understand what she saw—that was how much of her mind Folly Broadmore had beaten out of her.

"When Señor Weyburn realized what he had done, he knew he had to hide the murder. He decided to burn the house down, to make it seem Folly Broadmore had died in the fire. But there was still Magart Broadmore to deal with. Señor Weyburn couldn't marry her for fear that his own marriage would be discovered, and for fear that people would realize he had been carrying on a love affair with a married woman. Señor Weyburn had plans to run for sheriff as soon as Till Cooke stepped down, and he couldn't afford scandal.

"And so they decided there was nothing to be done but to make it appear she had died with her husband. That way Señor Weyburn could take her secretly into his own home, and live with her as a man lives with his wife. And so Floyd Fells murdered a Tonkawa woman, and they dressed her body in some of Magart's clothing, and burned the house down with her corpse lying near that of Broadmore. The trick worked; everyone believed that both Folly and Magart Broadmore had died in the fire.

"My husband and I had to be told some of what had happened, because it fell to us to take care of Magart Broadmore—though Señor Weyburn wished us to call her 'Mrs. Weyburn.' My husband was told more than I was . . . they trusted him more, because they could tell he was more like them than I was. They were right. My husband is an evil coward, and he doesn't know I have come here tonight. I hope never to see him again.

"I knew there were things I hadn't been told, and I begged my husband to tell me. At last he did, and then I wished I hadn't been told at all. The evil of what had been done, and the evil Eduardo and I were doing in helping hide it, was too much for me. I had to tell someone, and at last I did. It was only Paco, a simple old beggar who would go from ranch to ranch looking for food or something to steal."

"So that's how Paco knew!" Keller cut in.

"Yes, Señor Keller. And then it only grew worse. I realized that Magart had become with child—Señor Weyburn's child. I began to fear what would become of the child once it was born, because I knew it would mean the end of all secrets unless it was sent away or done away with. I decided then that when the time of birth came, I would somehow get the child to safety. And so I have brought it here to you, Señor and Señora Keller. And I throw myself onto your mercy, because I don't know what will become of me, now that I've betrayed Señor Weyburn."

Keller stood, holding the baby out before him and looking into its little face. He remained silent for a long time. Then he turned to Maria. "You have nothing to fear from me, Mrs. Cruz. You have done the right thing in coming here. This baby is now safe, and so are you. But I have to leave. I'm going to Weyburn's house."

Claire stood. "Jed, you're not thinking of—"

"Don't worry, Claire. I doubt David Weyburn is anywhere within miles of here now. I'm going to claim the body of my sister, if he hasn't done away with it already."

29

The funeral and burial service for Magart Keller Broadmore drew one of the largest crowds in the county's history. The story of David Weyburn's deception, and the tragedy of Magart's death and the other aspects of the remarkable story, made all the rounds, and even drew the attention of the newspapers from the big cities.

One portion in particular seemed to be told the most frequently and with the most dramatic flair: that being the way Jed Keller had found the body of his sister. After hearing Maria Cruz's revelations, he had ridden to the Weyburn house and found it deserted and dark—dark, that is, except in the upper bedroom, where a score of candles and lamps burned around the bed upon which Magart's still body lay. Weyburn had closed her eyes and laid her straight, and in her hands had placed a bouquet of dried flowers taken from a vase downstairs. With the flowers was a note, written in his own hand: *Forgive me.*

Weyburn was nowhere to be found, though he was sought extensively throughout and all around the county. He, like his servant Eduardo Cruz, had vanished, no doubt having fled far away.

"He was afraid of the Old Boys," some speculated at Magart's graveside. Others said his fear was more probably caused by Calvin McBrearty, who was reportedly about to bring damning information about Weyburn before the next grand jury. One of the charges, according to the general wisdom, would be an accessory to murder charge involving the death of Winnie, the murdered Tonkawa woman, and possibly another related to the slaying of Paco the Mex.

Many, both private citizens and press, sought to question Jed Keller about the unique events he had found himself in the middle of. He answered no queries. Keller had no desire to discuss the matter, and it was evident that his grief was deep both for his sister and for his friend Charlie Lilly. The background of Lilly's death was a matter of speculation among the people. Information about the fight at the remote Brock Spring had been kept out of public circulation by McBrearty and the few others who knew of it, so no one was really sure Lilly's fatal wounding had come during an Old Boy excursion. Still, rumors flew.

Jed Keller called on Calvin McBrearty two days after Magart's burial in the city cemetery—Keller had forbid that she be buried on the ranch grounds beside Folly Broadmore—to ask him his views on the likelihood of David Weyburn ever being brought to justice.

"Eventually he'll turn up, somewhere," McBrearty said. "Frankly, I'm surprised he even fled—I didn't think he would do it. Otherwise I'd have never—" He cut off.

"Go on."

McBrearty sighed and tugged the left side of his mustache. "I may have made an error of judgment. I told Weyburn that I was planning to bring evidence against him before the grand jury."

"For land's sake, McBrearty! Why the devil—"

"Don't jump down my throat, Keller. At the time, I knew nothing about Magart, or the Tonkawa woman's death. And it was certain that Weyburn had already heard that charges would probably come against him. The man had a big home and a sizable ranch investment. The idea of him running away from all that seemed inconceivable. And quite honestly, I still don't believe he would have left if Magart had not died. I think he would have stayed at her side. Whatever his flaws—and they were legion—Weyburn apparently was devoted to Magart. He committed murder because of her, for God's sake."

"Weyburn is an odd mix," Keller conceded. "On the one hand he killed the husband who had beaten her nearly to death—then on the other, he locked her away and denied her the care she needed in childbirth. He took a personal risk to save my own neck by locking me up the night of the Brock Spring fight, but at the same time he allowed two of my best friends in the world to ride to their deaths under Cutter Wyeth's guns. He proved himself devoted to Magart, just like you said, but he also let Floyd Fells murder an innocent Indian woman just to cover his own guilt. And it was Weyburn who let Cutter Wyeth go free, and because of that, Till Cooke was murdered." Keller paused thoughtfully. "I guess when you weigh him in the balance, there's not enough good to offset the bad. And what good he had was generally tainted with his own selfishness."

"Jed, I vow to you: If Weyburn can be found and brought into court, I'll do my best to see him dealt with to the fullest extent possible."

Keller smiled coldly. "If it's me who finds him, you won't have to worry about prosecution, McBrearty. All you'll have to do is send out for a good pine box and a grave digger."

"It might be counted a foolish thing to voice such a threat right in front of the county prosecutor," McBrearty said.

"It might—but it's far from the first foolish thing I've done," Keller said.

"I'm serious about this, Keller. I've overlooked a lot with you. But you listen to me: I'm sworn to uphold the law, and there's only so many things I can turn my back on. Don't get some fool notion of going after Weyburn yourself, or Wyeth either, for that matter."

Keller stared right into McBrearty's eyes. "I used to talk about leaving the law in the hands of the official lawmen myself, you may recall. A man named Till Cooke gave me a new perspective on that. He taught me that sometimes a man has to deal with wrongdoing in a direct way. Charlie Lilly believed that too."

"And Till Cooke and Charlie Lilly are both dead. Don't become a loose cannon on the deck, Keller. That'll do no good for you, me, this county, or the memory of your sister. Take that as a warning."

"Warning heard. Now if you'll excuse me, I've got to go down and meet the stage. Charlie Lilly's brother's coming in today to see to his things, few though they were."

"Give him my condolences."

"I will."

"Jed Keller, you heed what I've said—hear?"

"Good-bye, McBrearty. See you around."

He left the district attorney's office and strode down the street toward the stage office, hands in the pockets of his mackinaw. McBrearty stood at his window, watching him go, and tugged at his mustache so hard that it hurt.

That night, Claire noticed that Jed Keller was quiet and somber. He had been like that since Magart's death, but tonight he was unusually so. In their bed, she put her arms around him and asked him what was on his mind.

"I talked to Charlie Lilly's brother today," he said. "He came in to claim Charlie's things and to pay his respects at the grave."

"I knew he was due in soon."

"He told me something . . . I don't quite know how to feel about it."

"What was it?"

"Ed Lilly—that's his name—he's a lot like Charlie was. Clever and keen, you know. We talked, and I told him I intended to see Wyeth and Weyburn pay for what they've done, and pay by my own hand if at all possible. What he told me sort of shook me up, I admit."

Now Claire was intrigued. She pushed up on one elbow and looked into Keller's face. "What did he say?"

"He told me not to try and avenge Charlie. He said he understood what I was feeling, because he'd been through it himself. Seems he and Charlie had a younger brother once, a simple fellow. He got killed in an accidental shooting."

"That's sad."

"It's more than that, Claire. That shooting happened in a Missouri bank where this young fellow worked, and the man who shot him was a greenhorn deputy."

"Jed . . . he was talking about you!"

"He was, though he didn't know it. He said that for a long time after his brother died, he was determined to kill that deputy in payback for the death. It was Charlie who talked him out of it. Said it wasn't worth it, and that it was just an accident, after all. Charlie told him that the poor fellow who shot their brother likely would suffer more punishment in his own mind than any avenger could inflict. He was right. God have mercy, he was right." Keller choked up as he talked. "Claire, Charlie Lilly went to his grave never knowing he was working for the very man who shot his brother all those years back. I never talked to him in any specific way about what had happened to me back in Missouri. I'm glad now that I didn't." Keller wiped at his face. "You know, the first time I saw Charlie, I knew there was something familiar in his face. It was the family resemblance to that fellow I shot. That's what it was. The family resemblance."

Claire held her husband for a while. "Jed, do you think that maybe what Charlie said to his brother might apply to this situation too?"

"You mean about Weyburn's mind inflicting more punishment than what I could give in vengeance? Maybe so, Claire. He must have loved Magart a lot, in his own selfish way. He's got to feel responsible for her death. Remember the note he left on her body? 'Forgive me,' it said."

"Maybe you should just let it go, Jed. Let Weyburn pay for what he did in his own way."

"Maybe . . . but what about Wyeth? There's no conscience in that man at all."

"Leave it be, Jed. Leave it be. Maybe he'll be required to pay too."

"But how?"

"I don't know. But just leave it be. I lost my uncle Till after he decided that it was up to him to settle all the scores and right all the wrongs. I see more and more of him in you. I don't want to lose you like I lost him. Just let it be, Jed. Please."

He leaned over and kissed her. "I think maybe I will, Claire. I think maybe I will."

30

Weeks rolled past, and the year of 1876 came to a close. Often Jed Keller thought about David Weyburn, out there roaming free somewhere while the woman who had borne his child lay in her grave; and about Cutter Wyeth, living his worthless life with the blood of Till Cooke on his hands. The thoughts would bring him fury, and he would consider going to search for them. But he never did. He didn't know where to look, for one thing. And he wasn't even sure anymore that it was his place to look, for another. The thing that Charlie Lilly's brother had told him had greatly tempered his thirst for vengeance.

Meanwhile, Magart's little baby boy thrived and grew. It was the image of Magart herself, and Keller was glad of that, because it made it easier to forget that David Weyburn was the father. The Kellers grew to love the baby, and named him Charles Doyle Keller, in memory of Charlie Lilly and Doyle Boston.

Maria Cruz remained in town, and occasionally came to visit the baby. The Kellers held no hard feelings toward her for her part in helping Weyburn cover his many sins; if not for Maria's honesty and courage at the end, the truth might have never come out. Maria struck a deal with Calvin McBrearty to serve as chief prosecution witness against Weyburn, should he ever come to trial, in exchange for her own immunity. Meanwhile, she found employment as a cook and maid at the Big Dakota, began attending almost every mass at the local Catholic church, and seemed to be a happier woman than she had been in a long time. As for Eduardo Cruz, he never appeared again. Maria grieved over him some, but as time passed, that pain lessened significantly.

The Old Boys rode no more after the Brock Spring incident. Their work, however, had already been substantially done. Stock theft had declined significantly, and after the disappearance of David Weyburn, it fell off even more. His hands deserted the ranch—several of them plundering the big stone house on their way out—and the court seized his property. McBrearty took every step possible to prepare for a thorough prosecution, but as time went by, anticipation of David Weyburn ever being seen again around Cade finally waned.

Keller was never called upon to face charges stemming from his vigilante activities, and for that he owed the sheer grace of McBrearty. Like almost everyone else around Cade, McBrearty knew Keller had certainly been part of the Old Boys, but he was quick to point out that he had no legal proof of it. Keller had never admitted outright to it, and all the incident of his jailing by Weyburn proved was that Weyburn *believed* Keller to be an Old Boy, not that he in fact *was* an Old Boy.

When the spring of 1877 swept in, matters changed for Keller. A newly hired cowhand fresh in from Kansas offhandedly commented that the infamous Cutter Wyeth had been taken into custody in Dodge City a few days before, right at the time he was leaving. Interestingly, Wyeth was wounded at the time he was arrested.

Keller asked if a lawman had wounded Wyeth. No, the cowboy replied. It was another fellow who had been riled by Wyeth. He had gotten away without being caught.

Keller was stirred by this new reminder of Wyeth. He lay awake most of the night, thinking back on his younger days with Cooke, and about the tragic way Cooke had died. He thought about Doyle Boston and Charlie Lilly too, riding into Wyeth's ambush at Brock Spring.

The next morning Keller informed Claire that he was going to Dodge City. He had to see if Wyeth was actually in custody, and do what he could to make sure he faced justice for the killings he had committed.

Claire was sad to see her husband's obsession renewed. At the same time, she knew there was no point in trying to sway him. She kissed him and told him she would pack him some good clothes to wear while he was in town.

The next morning he set off.

Jed Keller had never laid eyes on Dodge City until the morning he rode into it. Not much to see, really, especially given its wild reputation. It was pretty much just another frontier plains town. Keller had expected nothing else; he knew the tendency of Americans to develop overblown images of places with reputations . . . sort of the reverse of the way he had developed such a positive image of Cade before he first saw it.

Keller found himself a room at the Dodge House and headed out into the streets. Already the town was preparing itself for the arrival of the herds from the south. The saloons and faro houses and dance parlors were being cleaned and painted, and signs going up here and there announced higher prices on liquor, beer, and cigars. Keller only half observed it all; the only thing he was concerned about was finding Cutter Wyeth and having a talk with the county sheriff to assure that he was aware of Wyeth's crimes in Texas.

An hour later Keller was walking the streets again, with such an expression of anger on his face that two women actually crossed the street rather than pass him on the same boardwalk. He had just talked to the county sheriff, a man named Charles Bassett, and heard news that distressed him.

Cutter Wyeth, with his seemingly unending luck, had escaped. Bassett was embarrassed and angry over how it had happened, for Wyeth, he felt, had played him for a fool.

"He had a wound when we took him in," Bassett had said. "A gunshot, just a shallow furrow on his leg. Oh, but he moaned about it something fierce, declaring it was mortifying on him. He begged to be put in the care of a doctor, and finally I had my fill of his mouthing and sent him off to be patched. Well, he clouted my deputy and got away clean. It's a shameful thing he was able to do it so easy, and I'm embarrassed to be telling you."

Keller found the news depressing. There truly was no justice when men such as Till Cooke and Charlie Lilly died, while scum such as Wyeth couldn't even be held in custody. There was no changing what had happened, though. Keller had to be satisfied simply to tell Bassett about Wyeth's killings in Texas and ask that word be wired immediately to District Attorney General Calvin McBrearty's Cade office if Wyeth should be recaptured.

"Who was it that shot Wyeth, by the way?" Keller had asked Bassett. An odd and intriguing possibility had just crossed his mind.

"A redskin," Bassett answered. "Wyeth was giving him some sort of devilment, and he had his fill of it, I reckon. Why you ask?"

"Just wondering, that's all. Thank you, Sheriff Bassett."

Well, that was it. He had traveled this far merely to be disappointed. Keller decided to remain only one night and begin his ride home the next morning. There was plenty to do back in Texas—cattle to round up and brand, and a trail drive to engage later.

At the moment, the most important business was filling his stomach, however. Keller headed back for the Dodge House down on a corner of Front Street. He entered the restaurant, seated himself, ordered a steak and coffee, and settled back to read a copy of a local newspaper somebody had left on the chair beside him.

He read for about ten minutes, then lowered the paper. At the same moment, another man across the room from him went through an identical motion, lowering his own newspaper. Keller was situated so as to look him squarely in the face. He gasped and stood.

It was David Weyburn.

A wild jumble of feelings rolled through Keller. Before him, and just now seeing him in turn, was the one man he had come to believe he would never see again. Weyburn stared back at Keller with wide eyes and a pallid face.

Keller strode forward and came to a stop just beside Weyburn's chair.

"Keller . . . I didn't expect to see you here."

"And I didn't expect to see you, Weyburn." He inspected the despised man closely. "You look like pure hell. You been sick?" Indeed Weyburn did look bad. Downright terrible, as if he had just checked out of a deadhouse, as most folks still sardonically termed hospitals.

Weyburn didn't seem interested in answering. "I suppose you're thinking you might kill me."

"Well, Weyburn, I'm impressed. You've become quite a mind reader. You ought to turn it into an act and book yourself into one of the local show halls."

"I don't blame you for hating me, Keller," Weyburn said. "God knows I've learned to hate myself. I didn't want her to die, you know. I truly did love her."

"You locked her away like she was no more than a dog in season. You left her to go through her travail alone, when a doctor might have saved her."

"The servants were supposed to come for me when she began to have the baby," Weyburn said. "It wasn't my fault they didn't do what I told them."

"You don't fault yourself? Then why do you hate yourself over it, like you say you do?"

Weyburn lowered his head. "Because I do fault myself, truth be told. I failed her. I should have . . . but it's too late now."

"Indeed it is. And it is your fault, Weyburn. Just like it's your fault that Till Cooke was murdered."

"That was Cutter Wyeth's doing—I had nothing to do with that!"

"Other than turning Wyeth loose so he was free to do it, you should say! And I fault you the same for what happened at Brock Spring."

"You owe me your life for that one, Keller, and you know it! If I hadn't locked you up, you would have ridden right into the same ambush."

"Maybe so—but don't expect me to thank you for any favors. You let two good men, one of them in particular a fine friend of mine, ride to their deaths, all so they'd quit hanging the scum of your county and let you run your stock thieving ring without interference! And even if you did save my neck, it was to appease your rotten conscience for the way you locked away my sister like she was a sack of old potatoes."

Weyburn stood, drawing the attention of the others in the restaurant. "I was always good to Magart. I loved her! She was my wife!"

"Your wife? No, Weyburn. She was never your wife. More your prisoner, a captive kept for your pleasure."

Weyburn swung at Keller. Keller ducked and came up with his own punch, striking Weyburn in the jaw and knocking him back onto his seat.

A man in an apron came out of the kitchen, shotgun in hand. "Here, now—that's enough of that in here!

This is no south-of-the-tracks dive here! You men take it outside!"

Keller dug into his pocket, pulled out a few bills, and tossed them at the man. Then he grabbed Weyburn's collar and all but dragged him out of the saloon and down to the nearby railroad tracks. "Weyburn, if you want to take another swing at me, do it. Give me an excuse to beat you to death!"

But Weyburn seemed deflated and weak now. He slumped where he stood and let his hands hang limply at his sides. "I won't fight you, Keller. If you want to kill me, kill me. Save me the trouble of doing it myself."

Those words surprised Keller and took a little of the fight out of him. "What—you're trying to tell me you're some conscience-tortured soul or something?"

"That's exactly what I am. You think you know what it is to hate someone, Keller? Do you? I know about hate. I hate exactly the same man you do. I hate David Weyburn."

"You're making no sense."

"This life we live makes no sense, Keller. I've been low, then high, then low again, and wherever I am, I'm still the same foul piece of . . . but forget the talk. It makes no difference. You want to kill me, then kill me. Go ahead. I won't stop you."

Keller was flabbergasted; Weyburn really seemed to mean it. "I think you really are sick, Weyburn. You look like death itself."

"The look will fit soon enough. I wanted the chance to kill Cutter Wyeth first, but what does that matter, when it comes down to it? I'd still feel just as dirty."

"Wait a minute . . . you're saying you came to Dodge to kill Cutter Wyeth?"

"Yes. He's here, you know. Locked up in the county jail yonder at the courthouse."

"Not anymore. He got free. This time he had to work for it a little . . . he didn't have a partner as sheriff, you know, somebody who would just turn him loose and call it escape."

"Wyeth is gone?"

"That's right."

"So I've come here for nothing."

"Maybe not. Maybe fate brought you here, Weyburn. So I'd catch you. I'm taking you back to Cade with me. I want to see you stand trial on those indictments McBrearty has waiting for you."

Weyburn wasn't listening. "I'll bet I know where he is!" he said. His tone indicated the words were self-directed.

"You mean Wyeth?"

"Yes . . . let me go, Keller. Let me go find him. Let me kill him."

"Why the devil would you want to kill Cutter Wyeth? You expect me to really believe that?"

"Appeasement, Keller. Payback. Justice—the same kind of justice you and your Old Boys had in mind when you looped those signs around the necks of your victims. Don't you see, Keller? I have to set things right. Make everything square. Wyeth and me, we're two of a kind. We're both guilty . . . we've both got to pay."

Keller had a dawning awareness of a surprising but likely notion: David Weyburn was no longer fully sane. Something had been grinded down in the man until it finally gave way. The thought was so startling that Keller was left speechless a moment.

Weyburn looked at him with a fearfully inquisitive expression. Then he began to back away. A few steps back, he turned and headed down the street.

"Weyburn!"

Weyburn turned. Keller had drawn a pistol from beneath his jacket and leveled it. Weyburn licked his lips. "I can find Wyeth," he said. "I know some of his haunts—I can find him, and kill him."

Keller began to squeeze the trigger. At the same time his arm began to shake. He looked around. This was broad daylight, at the end of a public street. He couldn't gun down Weyburn here. He lowered the pistol. Who was he trying to fool? He couldn't have gunned down Weyburn if it were midnight and this was a back alley in China.

"All right, Weyburn. You find him, and I'm going to be right at your side."

31

Weyburn frowned. "You want to track down Wyeth
. . . with me?"

"That's right. I'm not fool enough to let you
out of my sight. If you're going after Wyeth, I'm going
with you. If you're serious about wanting to see him
punished, then I'll give you the chance to prove it."

Weyburn eyed the ground and looked discomfited.
He nodded. "All right. All right. If that's the way you
want it."

"Where are you staying?"

Weyburn said, "Right there," and thumbed back at
the Dodge House.

"Do tell! So am I. It's no wonder we ran across
each other, then. Go on—we're getting our gear and
heading out. Where do you think Wyeth is?"

"There's an old cluster of dugouts out east of here,
on the road that leads to a little town called Eldridge.
Wyeth has holed up there before."

"Then we'll pay us a little visit out that way."

They went to Keller's room first. There was little to
gather; Keller had packed only what would ride in his
saddlebags or rolled inside his bedroll. They went next
to Weyburn's room, and there Keller made his mistake.

Perhaps it was overconfidence or simply bad judgment, but he went to the window of the room and looked out onto Front Street while Weyburn gathered his own goods. Something warned Keller at the last moment, and he turned, but it was already too late. Weyburn had a pistol in his hand, already uplifted and swinging down. Keller tried to dodge and failed. The heavy barrel struck him across the brow and knocked him to the floor, his vision spinning, twisting, sparkling away into darkness.

When he came to, the shadows in the room were different. Not greatly so, but different. Time had passed. He dug out his watch as he pushed to his feet. An hour. A full hour had gone by.

He squinted against the pain in his brow and touched his head. At least he was alive. Weyburn could have killed him—and he wondered why he hadn't. Keller swore at himself. He had been quite a dunce to let this happen. Now he was disarmed and Weyburn was gone—probably off to join up with his old partner Wyeth and have a good laugh at how he had pushed over such a pile of fool truck on Jed Keller. All Weyburn's talk, all his professed grief and dirty conscience—it had all been a fraud. He should have known. It was likely that the real reason Weyburn had come to Dodge City was to try and get Wyeth out of jail. All that talk of guilt and punishment and setting things right . . . he had been almost ready to really believe it!

Keller looked for his saddlebags and bedroll; they were gone. Weyburn had taken not only his weapons, but everything else he had carried. Keller veered toward the door, still dizzy. He almost overran a man in the hall and a woman on the stairs before he made it out onto the street. He headed for the livery and took his horse from its stall. His saddle was locked up in a room to the side, and Keller rattled the door futilely, trying to open it. "Liveryman!" he yelled. "Where are you?"

The aging livery keeper emerged from an outhouse

out back of the stable. Still pulling galluses over his shoulders, he said, "Hold on, hold on—give a man a chance to answer, durn you!"

"I need my saddle. The name's Keller. Hurry!"

"All right, all right . . ."

The man moved too slow to suit Keller. He fidgeted and muttered under his breath as the fellow dragged out the saddle and heaved it onto Keller's waiting horse— not noticing that Keller was taking advantage of the moment to reach into the momentarily unlocked storage room and slip a pistol out of a gun belt that hung on a peg in the wall, stored there for safe keeping by some livery customer who intended to abide by Dodge's ordinances against carrying guns in town. Hooking a loaded pistol was a stroke of luck Keller had not anticipated. He stuck it under his belt, in the back.

As he tightened the cinch, the old liveryman looked up and eyed the reddish mark on Keller's forehead. "Looks like somebody walloped you right good, friend."

"They did," Keller said. He swung up onto the saddle. "Then they cleaned out my pockets and took everything I had."

"Wait a minute . . . you got no money?"

"Not at the moment. Don't you worry—I'll send it on from Texas." He urged the horse out of the stable before the old liveryman could stop him, and rode off down the street with the man yelling after him.

What he was doing was probably foolish, and he knew it. Surely Weyburn had lied about the place he expected to find Wyeth. Nevertheless, Keller was heading in that direction, just in case. There was certainly nothing else to do; Weyburn could have ridden out in any direction. He would follow the only lead he had, even if the odds of it being a good one were virtually nil.

Or maybe not. Maybe at the time Weyburn had talked about the dugouts on the Eldridge road, he had been telling the truth. Maybe he hadn't known at that point that he would have an opportunity to escape, and so had not bothered to lie. They were remote odds, but worth putting to the test. If the gamble paid off, he would be led to both Weyburn and Wyeth.

And given that he had only a pistol and six rounds of ammunition, he would probably have to make that opportunity work to his advantage—if he could at all.

An hour outside of Dodge, Keller began to pick up sign of a lone horseman riding ahead of him. It might be Weyburn—or it might be any other man in Kansas, for that matter. When the road divided and the tracks veered toward Eldridge, Keller was encouraged.

He became lost in the mid-afternoon, and by dusk felt he was no closer to finding the right way again. He had followed the horseman's track off the main road, gambling that the rider was in fact Weyburn, and then he had lost the trail altogether. Now, in gathering gloom, he gave up any hope of finding where Weyburn had gone.

He rode back in the direction of the main road. Tonight would be spent beneath the stars, blanketless, his head on his saddle. He didn't look forward to it. And he was terribly hungry.

He was about to stop when he saw the light. A distant flicker, as if a shutter had been opened and closed. Yet strain his eyes as he might, he saw no sign of a habitation out there. Perhaps it was too dark to make out the form of the house . . . or perhaps there was little form to make out. Perhaps this house was part of the earth itself.

"A dugout!" Keller said aloud. Immediately hunger and weariness were forgotten. He had found them—he was sure of it.

The light flickered again, and he rode toward it. When he was close enough to see that it was in fact a dugout, he dismounted and tethered his horse to a bush. It was almost totally dark now. He drew the pistol he had stolen—it was a Remington, unfamiliar and uncomfortable in his hand—and advanced. He heard a faint wickering and noted two horses in a pen behind the dugout. One was unfamiliar. The other was a black he had seen Weyburn riding many times.

He went to the window and looked in around the edge of the shutter. There, seated at a table with one hand holding a fan of cards and the other curled around a glass of whiskey, sat Cutter Wyeth. Across the table from him was David Weyburn, also drinking and playing cards. Wyeth was talking, telling some profane story or another. Weyburn was silent, and very somber, yet he didn't seem to be listening.

Keller examined Wyeth. He wore no gun belt, but his pistol lay on the table before him, within easy reach. Weyburn also was armed; his pistol was in his gun belt. Keller looked around the room as best his limited field of vision would allow. Against the wall and close to Weyburn he saw a familiar shotgun. Till Cooke's shotgun, the one Wyeth had stolen the night he murdered the old lawman.

The sight of the shotgun sent a fire through Keller. He gritted his teeth, hard. His fingers squeezed the grip of his pistol, harder. He stepped back three paces, advanced, and hammered the shutters into splinters with his foot.

It all happened in a blur of speed. Wyeth cursed in surprise and reached for his pistol. Keller raised his own pistol and aimed it through the window, yelling for the men inside to give up and not touch their weapons. The call made no difference. Keller was aware of Wyeth scooping up his pistol, and of Weyburn reaching for his own even as he stood, shoving his chair toward the wall behind him.

With a yell of fury Keller cocked his pistol and squeezed the trigger. Cutter Wyeth was in his sights. The hammer clicked; no explosion, no smoke and fire, no roar. The pistol was faulty. Keller backstepped, started to turn. Wyeth cursed again and fired. Keller felt some-

thing like fire rip through his torso, felt himself fall. At
the same time he saw David Weyburn lifting his pistol,
aiming it, firing it. Cutter Wyeth's head jerked as if
struck by a club, sent forth a red spray, and then the
outlaw pitched sideways and fell to the floor.

As Keller's world began to spin and darken, he
knew that Cutter Wyeth was dead, and that David Weyburn had killed him. Maybe he had been sitting at that
table waiting for the first good opportunity to do it, or
maybe his violent act had been just another case of
David Weyburn impulsively protecting the brother of
the woman he had loved. Keller had no chance to decide
that question. A numbing darkness crushed in against
him, seeped into the inside of his skull, and he knew no
more.

The next hours—days? weeks? Keller could not tell
—passed in a disjointed series of nightmarish images,
odd sounds, peculiar pains, and hellish music that came
from inside his brain. And then, one day, he was well
enough to know that he was still living, and in Dodge
City, and in a bed. There were faces of strangers, strangers who told him he was fortunate to be alive.

He asked how he got where he was, and they told
him a sandy-haired man had brought him in, then vanished. Keller knew it must have been David Weyburn.

He had them wire Claire and tell her he had been
hurt, but was now getting better and would be home
soon. And then he wrote her a detailed letter, telling her
that Cutter Wyeth was dead, that David Weyburn had
killed him, and how it all had occurred. He added that
they would almost certainly never lay eyes on Weyburn
again.

Claire wrote him back. Her letter said only that she
loved him, and was eager for his return, and was sending a couple of ranch hands to Dodge with a wagon to
bring him home as soon as he was fit to travel.

He rested and healed and counted the days.

*   *   *

It happened only two days after he was home again. Keller awoke in the night, hearing the dogs barking furiously. He rose and put on trousers, a shirt, and his boots, and went to the door. When he opened it, he found a shotgun leaned carefully against the door frame. It was Till Cooke's old shotgun, the one Cutter Wyeth had taken. Whoever had put it there had shined the maple stock to perfection and oiled and rubbed the double barrel.

The dogs were barking over across the rise, where the Broadmore house had stood, and where Folly Broadmore lay buried beside a Tonkawa woman named Winnie. Keller picked up the shotgun and walked in that direction. What he found was unexpected, but oddly, it didn't surprise him. How could anything David Weyburn did surprise him, given all that had already happened?

Weyburn's body swung from a mesquite tree, his feet no more than three inches above the ground. Lacking a rope, he had torn the sleeves from his shirt, tied them together to make a cord, and done the job with that.

The placard that hung against Weyburn's chest was lettered in his own hand, and all it said was: Justice.

ABOUT THE AUTHOR

Writing with power, authority, and respect for America's frontier traditions, CAMERON JUDD is a prolific young western writer who hails from Tennessee. Judd captures the spirit of adventure and promise of the wild frontier in his fast-paced, exciting novels. In the tradition of Max Brand and Luke Short, Cameron Judd is a new voice of the Old West.

A hero of his own time and for generations to come . . .

CROCKETT OF TENNESSEE
by
Cameron Judd

He was a common man of uncommon exploits. Cattle drover, bear hunter, husband and father, Indian fighter, soldier, politician, martyr. He rose from a dirt poor youth in the hardscrabble hills of Tennessee to earn the love of his countrymen and to strike fear in his enemies. Here is the story of Davy Crockett as it has never been told, a tale of triumph and tragedy—of an extraordinary man who at one time eyed the Presidency, but whose wanderlust and fate ultimately drew him west, to a small mission in Texas known as the Alamo.

Turn the page for an exciting preview of Cameron Judd's epic novel, CROCKETT OF TENNESSEE, on sale in July 1994, wherever Bantam Books are sold.

He heard the rumble of the wheels, smelled the horses, and finally saw the wagons. A long line of them, laden with casks, crates, and sacks, rolling slowly toward him.

David Crockett shifted to the side of the road and kept a steady pace, passing the wagon train. All the wagoners were strangers to him, but friendly enough, calling and waving, perhaps thinking it odd to see so young a traveler on foot alone.

David went on past; the train of wagons receded behind him. A glance at the sun and a rumble in his stomach told him it was nearly time to eat, and it crossed his mind that had he remained closer at hand, the wagoners might have offered an invitation for him to share their food, allowing him to stretch his own provisions farther. It was a selfish thought, to be sure, but a young fellow with less than four dollars to see him through hundreds of miles had to think selfishly to survive.

He decided to turn back and catch up with the wagon train, even though that would temporarily take him away from the direction he needed to go. A pretext of looking for a dropped knife would serve the purpose, he figured.

David's hopes were fulfilled. The wagoners had stopped for their meal by the time he reached them, and several friendly voices called for him to join them. There proved to be no need to invent a story about a lost knife.

David was seated with trencher on lap and bread in hand when a short, round fellow with a big grin splitting his ruddy face came to him, bearing his own laden trencher. With a grunt and mumble he settled his plump body down beside David, then stuck out his hand.

"Myers, Adam Myers," he said.

David swallowed his most recent bite of bread. "David Crockett."

"Crockett! I once met a Crockett in my home town. What was his name? John, I think. A constable or magistrate in Greene County, over in Tennessee. That's where I hail from. Greene Courthouse."

"John Crockett is my father."

"Law of Moses! What do you think of that? Where is your father these days? Bad fortune with that mill venture of his a few years back . . . I heard he had moved."

"Yes. He's in Jefferson County now, running a tavern for wagoners, over nearby Cheek's Crossroads."

"Well, I'm throwed, running across you out here. Alone and all, and young as you are."

David sensed that Myers was curious about his business, and volunteered, "I came with my older brother and some other folks, herding cattle. I'm on my way home; they'll be coming later."

"Oh. A cattle drover, are you? Have you ever worked with wagons?"

"I rode with a wagoner named Dunn for a short bit," David said. Myers nodded and lifted his brows, apparently assuming David meant he had worked with Dunn. David saw no need to correct the misunderstanding. He was beginning to catch the scent of a coming offer, and though he hadn't come looking for one, it couldn't hurt to hear out all the options.

Myers vindicated David's anticipation in his next sentence. "Young Mr. Crockett, perhaps you'd like to join my train," he said. "We're going to Gerardstown and after that will be returning to Tennessee. It wouldn't be much out of your way to come with us, and I'd pay you decent. I could use the help."

David weighed the possibility, and rejected it. "Thank you, Mr. Myers," he said. "But I reckon I'd best be getting on home."

As David walked on a half-hour later, his stomach nicely full, he told himself that he had gotten out of Myers all he had hoped for: a good, free meal. Still, Myers's invitation lingered in mind. And did he really need to get home, after all? Wouldn't it be as his brother had said: John Crockett holding his anger like a snapping turtle holding a toe? The drive to Front Royal had moved along at a fast clip, and David was making an even faster return journey. At this rate he would be home long before John Crockett had let go of his anger, and probably be worse off than before. And old Kitching would certainly have a thrashing of his own held in store for his wayward pupil.

David stopped, thought for a few moments, then turned. Myers's offer was seeming more enticing the longer he considered it. A side journey to Gerardstown would buy more time for tempers back home to cool, put an extra jingle in his pouch, and give him company and protection on the homeward journey, even if it did delay it.

He loped back to the wagon train. Myers greeted him with a grin and handshake. He seemed a jolly soul, the kind of employer who was a goodly companion as well.

David was sure he had made the right decision. He caught himself thinking that his father would be proud of him . . . but there was something uncomfortable about that idea, considering that it was his father he was running from, so he put the thought out of his mind.

"Well, I wonder who them folks are?" Adam Myers asked.

David was beside Myers on the wagon, shielding his eyes with his hand and peering hard at the approaching riders. "I can tell you who they are," he said. "That one on the roan horse is Jesse Cheek, and the fellow on the big black is my brother, James."

James Crockett wore a big smile by the time he was close enough for expressions to be visible. He had always been keen of eye, and had recognized David on the wagon while still far away.

"Dave, it's fine to see you," he said. "I ain't rested easy since you took off."

"I've done well enough," David replied.

"So I see—riding on a wagon instead of walking."

"Where's my brother?" Jesse Cheek asked.

"Way on toward home by now," David said. "We parted ways."

"You had a falling out?"

"No sir. Just parted ways." David didn't want to tell Cheek how his brother had hogged the saddle and left him to walk.

David introduced Myers to the others; hands were shaken on all sides. Myers said that he remembered having seen James back in Greene Courthouse when he was a much younger fellow. James said that

Myers looked familiar to him, too, then turned to David.

"Looks to me you're heading the wrong direction to go home," he said.

"I ain't going home, not yet," David responded. "I've hired myself out to Mr. Myers to go to Gerardstown. After that, we'll be coming back to Tennessee."

James frowned. "I don't know about that, David. The family will be fretting fierce over you by now. And if I go home and tell them it was me who helped you run off to begin with, and then that I let you head out with a bunch of wagoners—no offense to you, Mr. Myers—why, Pap'll probably take that hickory pole after me instead of you."

James's obvious intent was to stir David's feelings back toward home, but his mention of the hickory pole didn't help his case. David deeply feared the beating he was sure to receive.

"I've made Mr. Myers a pledge to work for him, at least as far as Gerardstown," David said.

"That's right," Myers added. He didn't seem so jolly now. James's attempts to lure away his employee apparently annoyed him.

James went at it hard. He reminded David of the time he had been away from home already, with none of the home kin knowing what had become of him. He talked of their sisters and mother, describing the tears they had surely shed over him and the prayers they must still be sending up for his safe return.

David was deeply affected by James's words, and to his own shame began to cry. A great homesickness stirred in him—but each time it welled up, the image of John Crockett and his hickory pole arose to counter it. No, David decided. He could not return, not yet. He told James to give word that he was well, and would be home as soon as his new work would allow it.

At last James accepted the inevitable, hugged his brother close, and patted his shoulders with both hands. He hurried away quickly, trying to hide his tears, but David saw them, and was wrenched.

He looked over his shoulder and watched James and his companions until they were out of sight. The wagons lurched forward, and David turned his gaze ahead.

At the moment, being a wagoner and far from home didn't seem to have much good about it at all, the threat of John Crockett's hickory stick notwithstanding.

They reached Gerardstown and disposed of their load. Afterward Myers sought a return cargo and could not find one. Eventually he heard of hauling work in another town, and went there. David did not follow, but remained in the Gerardstown area, working for a farmer, plowing and doing general labor, for twenty-five cents a day.

When Myers returned, David asked him if he was ready to return to Tennessee as planned, and discovered to his shock that Myers's scheme had changed. He still could find no return cargo to Tennessee, but he had located a profitable back-and-forth route between Virginia and Baltimore. For now, going home to Tennessee would have to wait.

Myers made the Virginia-Maryland run several times. David, in the meantime, continued laboring for the farmer, and saving his meager pay.

Spring came. David bought himself new clothing, sought out Myers and asked if he could accompany him to Baltimore. Myers had such a run planned, it turned out, one that would require only two wagons. He agreed, and David set off, seven dollars in his pocket, on a journey that would take him farther from home than he had ever been. Myers warned him of the dangers of the big city—theft on every hand, scoundrels who could spot a newcomer at a glance and fleece him of his money in moments. Might not David feel better about his seven dollars if Myers kept it for him? After all, Myers said, he was a businessman, accustomed to keeping and guarding money. David thought about it, and handed over his treasure.

An accident along the way caused damage to a wagon, and very nearly injury to David, who was almost crushed between the barrels of flour that made up the cargo. After shifting as many as possible of the barrels to the second wagon and making arrangements with a local farmer to store the rest until they could return to get it, they limped the rest of the way into Baltimore, and took the damaged wagon in for repairs that would take at least two days to complete. They went back and fetched the barrels they had stored with the farmer.

Then there was nothing to do but wait. David found himself with more time to explore the city than he had anticipated, and set out to explore it alone. Myers, who had grown moody since the accident, had seen it all before, and cared nothing about touring the town again.

Baltimore was a marvelous place to the young frontier boy. He had never seen so vast an expanse of buildings, nor so many people in one small area. He roamed the streets, gaping openly, seldom noticing the knowing grins he generated from the seasoned city folk who had seen such rural types blow through their town many times before.

What intrigued David most was the wharf and the great ships that lay in dock there. He stood in awe, staring at the tall masts, the intricate roping, the lapping water, the sails lined magnificently against the sky.

He watched as one particularly impressive ship sailed in and docked. Settling himself in a warm, sunny place, he watched the crewmen and dock hands emptying the holds. Curiosity arose, and he looked for and found an opportunity to slip aboard, very carefully, taking care to draw no notice.

Exploring the ship provided David more fun than he had experienced for the longest time. What a life this must be! He tried to imagine being aboard ship in the midst of ocean that stretched endlessly on all sides. Looking up the masts and the conglomeration of ropes and sail attached to them, he wondered what it would be like to crawl like a spider among it all, swaying and swinging high above the waves.

"And who may you be, young man?"

David wheeled and faced the speaker, a stranger dressed in a manner that marked him as the captain of the vessel. David's heart rose, pounding, feeling like it was trying to emerge from his throat. He assumed he was in great trouble.

"I'm . . . I beg your pardon, sir. I'll leave."

"What a voice! You have the sound of the western hills about you, my lad!"

The captain, on the other hand, had the sound of the Scottish hills in his own voice. That he was foreign only made him more intimidating to David. He backed away, turned, and headed for the ramp.

"Wait there, my boy," the captain said. "Let me have a look at you." He came closer, eyeing David evaluatively. "You're lean, but stout. I'd wager you can climb."

"I don't know, sir."

"Tell me about yourself. What work have you done?"

David, puzzled by the attention, briefly and rather clumsily mumbled a list of his various jobs. The captain rubbed his bearded chin thoughtfully, then said, "Might you consider a voyage to London?"

David was very taken aback. Was he being offered work? It certainly sounded that way. David was beginning to learn something about himself: He had some sort of natural quality, inexplicable to him, that made him appealing to others. He wondered if the captain was making a serious offer, but felt shy about asking. A misinterpretation would be embarrassing.

"Well, lad, what of it? Would you like to be a seafaring man?"

So he really *was* being offered a job. He didn't know what to think about such an unexpected, momentous proposition. He stammered and looked around—and a great sense of excitement rose all on its own, unanticipated and intense. His mind filled with images as big as the ocean itself—crashing waves, great and strange fish leaping from the water and descending again, dark shores coming closer, and cities filled with people whose faces and clothing and language was different than any he had heard before.

He looked up at the captain and nodded. "Yes sir. I believe I would."

The captain's name was McClure. He talked further with David, asking him about his parents and seeming pleased to learn they were far away in Tennessee. Did David mind the thought of being miles from his homeland and kin?

No, David replied. He had gotten past his homesickness, and wouldn't mind sailing all around the world if he got the chance. And as he said it, it was fully true. In the tearful parting with his brother weeks before, he had passed an emotional milestone. He still loved his kin, still felt fondly about his homeplace, but having made the break he didn't feel as bound to it as before, especially considering a prospect as exciting as this one. Right now the idea of being a seafarer was on him as strong as if it had been a lifetime ambition instead of a totally new notion.

McClure instructed David to go fetch his clothing and goods, and to return as soon as possible. Burning with the thrill of a new way of life—an ocean voyage! London!—David raced back to the inn where he and Adam Myers had taken lodging.

He found Myers half drunk and thoroughly transformed because of it. When David entered, Myers turned a glowering red face to him. "Where you been, boy?"

"To the wharf. I spoke to a ship's captain—he's offered me work on the ship. He says I can sail to London . . ."

Myers paused, taking it in, then snorted in contemptuous laughter. "London, is it? You? Why, they'd tire of you so fast they'd feed you to sharks before you were out of sight of land! You wouldn't know how to do a seaman's job!"

David was startled and puzzled by the new, dark side of Myers now revealing itself to him. "Well, whatever you think about it, it's what I want to do. I've come for my clothes and my money," he said.

"Have you? Well, you'll have neither."

"They're mine!"

"And you are in my hire, and under my care. You can put aside any notions about ships and ocean voyages. You're going nowhere but back to Tennessee. I've got a return load at last, ready to be hauled out as soon as the wagon is fixed."

David was crestfallen—then, in mounting stages, angry. "You're not my father, nor my owner. I want my money!"

"Well, you ain't having it."

"Give it to me!"

"I'll give you the back of my hand!" Myers groped around. "Where's that dratted bottle? Ah, here she is!" He took a long swig.

David raised his fist. "Where is my money? Give it to me!"

"Maybe I done spent it."

"You lie!"

Myers stood, wobbled toward David, and took a swing that missed.

"I want my money!"

"No—now get yonder into that bed, and stay where I can see you."

"No!"

Myers reached down to his boot and pulled out a knife. He waved it toward David. "Get into that bed, so I can keep a watch and make sure you don't sneak off on me."

David knew enough about drunks to realize it wouldn't be wise to challenge Myers while he was armed. Further, his anger was fading into despair, and he was losing the will even to argue. He went to the bed and fell into it, thinking of the ship, and the waiting captain, and his disappearing hope of a voyage to London.

It was late afternoon, and by the time the sun was setting, David had fallen asleep. When he awakened, Myers was slumped in a chair beside the door, the knife still in his grip. David stood and thought about trying to slip past him, but Myers lifted his head and looked straight at him in silence. Perhaps it was a move made in the midst of sleep, or perhaps not. David crawled back into his bed.

Myers kept a watch over him very closely all the next morning, and then throughout the day. David had hoped that as Myers's drunkenness went away, so would his ill will. This didn't happen. It seemed that Myers meant it when he said he considered David his personal charge.

A day later the wagon was fixed. David and Myers loaded up with the wares bound for Tennessee, and set out, David's wagon in front where Myers could keep an eye on him at all times.

Days passed. David's anger at the way Myers had treated him, and cheated him out of his money, lingered and grew, and he longed for escape. No opportunity came. Myers watched him doggedly. His harsh attitude clung to him, and David wondered what was wrong with the man. Had he encountered some sort of trouble in Baltimore that had soured him, but which David knew nothing about? It was a mystery David Crockett would never solve. Whatever the reason, Myers was now as gruff and unpleasant as he had been jolly in the past.

Early one morning, well before daybreak, David rose, gathered his clothing and a little food, and set out on foot. He had no money, nothing of value at all except the little scrap of silver his Uncle Jimmy had given him. If it came to it, he decided, he would exchange the silver for food and goods—but only if there was no other way to survive. The token remained precious to him in a way that outstripped monetary value.

Alone, cheated, and sad, David Crockett walked silently through the darkness, going nowhere but away from Adam Myers. His mind was miles away, aboard a tall ship, crossing the vast ocean toward London—a place that now, he was confident, he would probably never have the chance to see.

CAMERON JUDD

THE CANEBRAKE MEN

Following the War of Independence against the British, a band of Tennessee settlers intends to carve out a new state. But they face the opposition of the federal government, as well as bloody resistance from the Chickamauga Indians. In this untamed land Owen Killefer will find within himself a spirit as stout and strong as that of any rough-hewn frontiersman.

From one of America's most powerful and authentic frontier storytellers comes a sweeping new saga capturing the vision, the passion, and the pain that gave rise to a glorious new nation—America. This is the unforgettable story of the bold men and women who led the way into an unexplored land and an unknown future, seeking new challenges.

RECEIVE A FREE LOUIS L'AMOUR
WALL CALENDAR JUST FOR PREVIEWING
THE LOUIS L'AMOUR COLLECTION!

Experience the rugged adventure of the American Frontier portrayed in rich, authentic detail with THE LOUIS L'AMOUR COLLECTION. These riveting Collector's Editions by America's bestselling Western writer, Louis L'Amour, can be **delivered to your home about once a month.** And you can **preview each volume for 15 days RISK-FREE** before deciding whether or not to accept each book. If you do not want the book, simply return it and owe nothing.

These magnificent Home Library Collector's Editions are bound in rich Sierra brown simulated leather—**manufactured to last generations!** And just for previewing the first volume, you will receive a **FREE Louis L'Amour Wall Calendar** featuring 13 full-color Western paintings.

This **exclusive offer** cannot be found in bookstores anywhere! **Receive your first preview Collector's Edition by filling out and returning the coupon** below.
